Wow, What A Man.

Irish watched Kyle's long-legged gait as he walked away from her. The man was as handsome as buttered sin. She'd never met anyone in her life who oozed such sex appeal. And from the little that they had talked, she felt certain he would be lots of fun to be with.

He probably had everything a woman could ask for. Except money.

Why is it, if it's just as easy to love a rich man as a poor one, that I'm always attracted to the ones who don't have two nickels to rub together?

Irish sighed. She couldn't afford to let herself get sidetracked. Her plans were made; her bank account was committed. She was out to snare a millionaire.

And it was a crying shame that she was so captivated by Kyle Rutledge.

D0949235

Dear Reader,

There's something for everyone this month! Brides, babies and cowboys…but also humor, sensuality…and delicious love stories (some without a baby in sight!).

There's nothing as wonderful as a new book from Barbara Boswell, and this month we have a MAN OF THE MONTH written by this talented author. *Who's the Boss?* is a very sexy, delightfully funny love story. As always, Barbara not only creates a masterful hero and smart-as-a-whip heroine, she also makes her secondary characters come alive!

When a pregnant woman gets stuck in a traffic jam she does the only thing she can do—talks a handsome hunk into giving her a ride to the hospital on his motorcycle in Leanne Banks's latest, *The Troublemaker Bride.*

Have you ever wanted to marry a millionaire? Well, heroine Irish Ellison plans on finding a man with money in *One Ticket to Texas* by Jan Hudson. A single mom-to-be gets a new life in Paula Detmer Riggs's emotional and heartwarming *Daddy by Accident.* And a woman with a "bad reputation" finds unexpected romance in Barbara McMahon's *Boss Lady and the Hired Hand.*

Going to your high-school reunion is bad enough. But what if you were voted "Most likely to succeed"…but your success at love has been fleeting? Well, that's just what happens in Susan Connell's *How To Succeed at Love.*

So read…and enjoy!

Lucia Macro

Lucia Macro
Senior Editor

Please address questions and book requests to:
Silhouette Reader Service
U.S.: 3010 Walden Ave., P.O. Box 1325, Buffalo, NY 14269
Canadian: P.O. Box 609, Fort Erie, Ont. L2A 5X3

JAN HUDSON
ONE TICKET TO TEXAS

SILHOUETTE *Desire*

Published by Silhouette Books

America's Publisher of Contemporary Romance

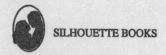

SILHOUETTE BOOKS

RECYCLED PAPER

ISBN 0-373-76071-X

ONE TICKET TO TEXAS

Books by Jan Hudson

Silhouette Desire

In Roared Flint #1035
One Ticket to Texas #1071

JAN HUDSON,

a winner of the Romance Writers of America RITA
Award, is a native Texan who lives with her husband in
historically rich Nacogdoches, the oldest town in Texas.
Formerly a licensed psychologist, she taught college psy-
chology for over a decade before becoming a full-time
author. Jan loves to write fast-paced stories laced with
humor, fantasy and adventure, with bold characters who
reach beyond the mundane and celebrate life.

Prologue

"**I**n your dreams, Buster!" Irish Ellison slammed the front door and stalked back to the den of the Foggy Bottom town house where her two roommates sat watching TV. *"Men,"* she groused, toeing off her high heels and plopping down on the couch next to Olivia.

"I take it that you and the senator's staffer are having some problems," Olivia said, offering Irish the popcorn bowl.

"You take right." She plunged her hand into the buttery kernels and popped a few in her mouth. "The jerk."

"What's wrong?" Kim asked. "Gavin seemed very nice. I thought the two of you had something going."

"I thought so, too—until he hit me up for a loan.

Can you believe it? The skunk takes me to a couple of embassy parties, wines and dines me with free booze and free food, and then tries to borrow money from me.''

Kim's eyes grew even larger behind her thick glasses. "He *didn't?*"

"He did. He's behind on his alimony."

"I didn't even know that Gavin had been married," Olivia said.

"Neither did I." Irish propped her feet on the coffee table. "Until tonight. Seems that he's been married not once, but twice, and he has four kids. Why do I always end up with somebody else's rejects? You're the psychologist, Olivia. What's my problem?"

Olivia, the oldest of the three—and considered the wisest—raised her brows at the former model who had legs up to her armpits, bone structure that most women would die for and a shining fall of hair that was naturally a magnificent shade somewhere between strawberry blond and copper. "I don't have my Ph.D. yet, but as far as I can tell, you don't have any major problems, Irish. It's this town. Washington has a dozen gorgeous single women vying for every available man—and even some that aren't available. If you're interested in meeting men, you've picked a bad place to settle."

"I didn't pick D.C. I'm only here because the jobs were drying up in New York and Aunt Katie left me this house. Maybe we'd better all move to Alaska. I understand that guys there are desperate for women."

Neither Olivia nor Kim mentioned the third reason that Irish had fled the Big Apple.

"I'm not interested in meeting men," Olivia said. "Been there. Done that."

Irish turned to the TV where Marilyn Monroe filled the screen. "What are we watching?"

"How to Marry a Millionaire," Kim said.

"Now there's an idea that appeals to me. My mama always said, 'It's just as easy to fall in love with a rich man as a poor one.'"

"I thought that your father was a butcher."

Irish waved off the comment. "Mama was a slow learner." Her eyes narrowed, and she leaned forward, staring at a young Lauren Bacall. "I didn't have her kind of luck in New York. I wonder where one goes nowadays to find millionaires—the kind that are good-looking, single and itching for a meaningful relationship?"

"Texas."

Irish and Olivia turned to Kim, who at twenty was the youngest member of the household. "Texas?" they echoed in unison.

"Sure. My...boss is a millionaire and from Texas."

"But your boss is a woman. Remember, Congress-*woman* Ellen O'Hara."

"Yes, but she has a couple of younger brothers *and* two cousins who are single and rolling in dough."

"Fat and bald, right? And short?"

Kim grinned. "Nope. Not the ones I've seen. They're quite good-looking. And tall. Want me to borrow their photographs from the office and bring them home?''

"Not for me," Olivia said. "I'm not interested."

Irish sat up. "I am. I'll be thirty next February. I'd like to be snuggly settled into a nice Dallas mansion and driving a Beemer by my birthday. I'm sick of selling cosmetics at Macy's and trying to hustle free-lance articles on beauty tips to keep up the payments on my little car. Which one of her brothers is tall, dark and the richest and the most handsome?''

Kim cocked her head. "Well, that probably would be Jackson, but he doesn't live in Dallas. Although the cousins…''

"Enough said. Jackson it is. How do I meet this guy?''

Olivia looked aghast. "You can't be serious. You wouldn't judge a potential husband simply by the size of his bank account.''

"I wouldn't? Pray tell, why not?''

"What about love?" Kim asked. "What about *passion?*''

"What about it? Passion is vastly overrated. I want security in my old age. Besides, I find money *very* sexy." Irish glanced at the movie, then watched intently for a few minutes. As the story unfolded, wheels and gears spun to life in her head. With a devilish gleam in her eyes, she turned to her roommates and said, "We need to map out a strategy.''

One

When Irish Ellison rattled the padlocked chain on the gate and it didn't budge, her spirits sank deeper than the high heels of her new suede boots into the soft ground.

"Drive through the gate and continue for another half mile," Ellen Crow O'Hara's secretary had said. But how the heck was she supposed to drive through a locked gate?

Thoroughly disgusted, Irish picked her way back to the Mercedes she'd rented over two hours before at the airport in Dallas. Things weren't turning out the way she'd planned at all. She'd gone for broke on the scheme she and her roommates had hatched. She'd maxed out her credit card on a seductive wardrobe and had wrangled an advance from an editor friend at *Esprit* for an article about young Texas millionaires at play. The advance had covered her ticket to Texas and the car rental. Her food and lodging at Crow's Nest, Jackson Crow's golf retreat beyond the locked gate and in the middle of nowhere, were supposed to be compliments of Ellen's brother.

Or so the secretary had said.

Her stomach growled. Lunchtime.

Had she made a wrong turn somewhere?

She had no alternative except to go back the way she'd come and find a phone. After several minutes of muttering and maneuvering, she turned the car in the narrow space and retraced her route to the highway. There wasn't a single house in sight, only thickly wooded areas interspersed with grassy fields dotted with big machines that looked like giant black grasshoppers bobbing their heads up and down.

When she reached the highway intersection, Irish turned into the parking lot of a quaint log building. The sign over the front door proclaimed: Cherokee Pete's Trading Post. In smaller letters it said: Grocery Store, Indian Museum, and Tourist Tepees, Pete Beamon, Prop.

To the left of the log building were four large, garishly painted tepees fashioned of something that looked like stucco or cement. Irish wrinkled her nose at the tacky structures, got out of the Benz and went inside the trading post.

Not a soul was in sight. If you didn't count the wooden fellows in feathered headdresses.

"Yoo-hoo," she called.

Silence.

She ventured a few steps into the dim interior filled with cluttered shelves of merchandise, a refrigerated case and a long wooden bar. Toward one end of the room two tables with chairs sat near a potbellied stove, and assorted merchandise—from saddles to shovels to souvenirs and bushel baskets of sweet potatoes—filled almost every available space. "Anybody here?"

More silence.

Spooky silence.

Then a rapid rattling like distant castanets whispered through the air.

Suddenly apprehensive, she backed out of the place and closed the door quietly.

Irish stood on the long porch, feeling frustrated and contemplating her next move, when a whining noise to her right captured her attention. The sound seemed to be something like a motorbike, and it came from a log shed a few yards away from the trading post.

She headed in that direction, carefully making her way over the soft ground, tiptoeing to preserve her boots from further destruction. When she rounded the corner and could see inside the shed, she went dead still.

Her eyes widened and her heart almost leapt out of her chest when she saw the man standing there.

But this wasn't just any man. Dressed in only a

white cowboy hat, boots and low-slung jeans, he was about six and a half feet of blatant male pulchritude. The sinewy muscles of his arms and shoulders bunched and rippled as he wielded a small chain saw.

Never had a man affected Irish so immediately or so viscerally as this one did. Seductive masculinity pulsated from his core and cast an aura around him like the glow of a sizzling neon sign. She could only stand there, openmouthed and mute, and stare at him. At bits of sawdust caught in his light chest hair and at beads of sweat glistening on his spectacular pecs, on his lean, muscled abdomen where the skin glistened golden tan. His jaw was as finely carved as the huge wooden bear he worked on with the chain saw. Unbelievably handsome, he had wonderful high cheekbones, a perfect nose.

And his eyes...his eyes took her breath away as their mind-blowing blue bored into hers.

He lopped off one of the bear's ears.

"Damn!"

He killed the chain saw and laid it aside.

Mortified by the sudden amputation she'd caused, Irish said, "Oh God, I'm sorry I startled you. Now your thing is ruined."

"My thing?" he asked in a deep, sexy voice that resonated inside her from gut to womb to toes.

She felt her face heat. If she hadn't known better, Irish would have sworn that she blushed, but she hadn't blushed since she was in puberty. She gestured toward the rough carving. "The bear."

He flashed a blinding smile that, if she hadn't already been awe-struck, would have laid her low. He removed his goggles, repositioned his hat over his damp blond hair and patted the bear's head. "No problem. We'll just rename him Vince."

Mesmerized, she continued to gape at him as all sorts of switches were being thrown inside her body. "Vince?"

His smile broadened into a grin, and her heels slowly sank into the ground. Another few minutes of this man and not only would her boots be beyond repair, but she would be a mindless puddle in the sawdust.

"Vince," he said, his eyes as busy over her as hers were over him. "Vincent. Vincent Van Gogh."

Her brain didn't register. "Vincent Van Gogh?" she asked blankly.

"You know, the artist who chopped off his ear."

"Ohhh," she said, feeling like a dolt. "That Vince." Her gaze went to his chest again. His gaze must have mimicked hers for she felt her nipples suddenly pebble.

Stripping off his leather gloves, he grabbed a towel that hung on a nail and swiped it across his sweaty, bare skin. "What can I do for you?" he asked as he wiped away sawdust and a particularly intriguing rivulet of perspiration that she'd been watching as it trickled downward toward his navel.

"Do for me?" What a loaded question. As she noted his long, supple fingers, she could name at least a dozen things—all of them extremely intimate—that she would love for him to do for her.

He chuckled softly, and she felt that darned heat spread over her face. "You need some help?" he asked.

"Help? Oh, yes. Er...uh, are you Cherokee Pete?"

"Nope. Pete's my grandfather. I'm Kyle." He tossed the towel aside, grabbed his shirt and hurriedly donned it. "Kyle Rutledge."

"I'm Irish. Irish Ellison."

Kyle almost said, *I know,* but something stopped him. In his California practice, a dozen or more women had brought him her photograph from some magazine or another, wanting her nose or her cheekbones or that lush mouth of hers. Instead, he tipped his hat and said, "Pleased to meet you, Miss Ellison. How may I help you, ma'am?"

"Could you tell me if that's the road to Crow's Nest?" She gestured over her shoulder.

"Yes, ma'am. That's it."

"Oh, dear. I was afraid you were going to say that. I'm supposed to meet Jackson Crow, but the gate's locked."

Well, damn it all to hell! Here was one of the world's most gorgeous women in the flesh, one who rang his bell and had him standing to attention, and be damned if his cousin hadn't staked her out first. As usual, Jackson was the luckiest son-of-a-gun walking. "Jackson's gone."

Her astonishing emerald green eyes widened in alarm. "Gone?"

"Gone."

"But—but I have an appointment. I'm supposed to spend several days at the retreat working on an article. On him and the men in the young millionaire's club."

"You don't know Jackson?"

She shook her head. "Never met him."

Kyle relaxed. His smile returned. "He and that crazy bunch of his buddies decided to go to Dallas for the Cowboys game Sunday. They'll be back Monday."

"But this is *Friday*."

"They started the party a little early. You must have just missed them."

"Our appointment was for a couple of hours ago. My plane was late, and I had some problems at the car rental agency."

Kyle watched her chew the inside of her cheek and look worried. He had a fleeting urge to go after Jackson with an ax handle for causing those furrows to form between her perfectly arched eyebrows. "I wouldn't let it upset me. Jackson will be back Monday—if he's sober enough to fly."

"*Sober* enough— Does he drink a lot?"

He bit back a grin. There was no way that he was going to exalt Jackson in this lady's eyes. His cousin had all the women he could handle now. Kyle had seen this one first. "Like a fish. The man's a sot." *Sorry, cuz,* he said silently.

A shot rang out, and Kyle flinched, afraid for a moment that the powers-that-be were about to strike him dead for lying.

Startled, too, Irish jumped. "What was that?"

"That's just Grandpa Pete. He's in bed with a broken hip, and when he needs some help, he fires his pistol out the window."

"Wouldn't a bell be better?"

He grinned. "You don't know my grandpa. Come on up to the store with me while I see what he needs, and then we'll see what we can do to get your problem straightened out. It's about time for lunch. You hungry?"

"Famished."

"You like chili?"

"With beans?"

"Bite your tongue, woman. This is Texas. Only a Yankee would spoil a perfectly good pot of chili with beans. You a Yankee?" he drawled.

She laughed, and the throaty sound of it made him think of cool sheets and warm flesh. "I'm from Washington, D.C.," she said. "At least that's where I live now. I'm originally from Ohio, but I lived in New York for several years."

"New York *City?*" he asked with an exaggerated drawl. "Did you like that place?"

She shrugged. "For a while."

"That's the way I felt about California. I found out the hard way that Texas is the only place for me."

Inside the store, Kyle settled Irish at one of the tables. "Let me go check on Grandpa Pete, and I'll be back in a few minutes with the chili."

Irish watched his long-legged gait as he walked away and went up the stairs at the end of the bar. Wow, what a man. Handsome as buttered sin. She'd never met anyone in her life who oozed such sex appeal. And from the little that they had talked, she felt that he would probably be lots of fun to be with. He was as smooth as a river stone in putting her at ease.

She sighed. He probably had everything a woman could ask for. She looked around the dusty, junky store.

Except money.

Why is it, Mama, that if it's just as easy to love a rich man as a poor one, that I'm always attracted to the ones who don't have two nickels to rub together?

It was a crying shame that she was so captivated by Kyle Rutledge. Especially now.

She sighed again. She couldn't afford to let herself get sidetracked. Her plans were made; her bank account was committed. She was out to snare a millionaire.

And if Jackson Crow had a problem or two, well... one couldn't have everything.

Two

Sweat popped out on her upper lip. Irish ignored it and spooned another bite of chili into her mouth. After all, it was a free meal, and with less than twenty dollars left in her wallet, she couldn't afford to be choosy.

"Too hot for you?" Kyle asked.

"It's fine. Just fine." She gulped half a glass of iced tea.

With her tongue and her esophagus cringing at what was coming, she forced another bite into her blistered mouth.

Tears came to her eyes. She gulped the other half glass of tea and shook out an ice cube to suck on.

She glanced up at Kyle. He was frowning. "You don't have to be polite," he said. "It is too hot for you. Sorry about that. Grandpa Pete likes his chili fiery enough to singe the pin feathers off a chicken, and I've gotten used to it. Let me fix you something else. How about a bologna sandwich? I make a mean bologna sandwich.''

Relieved that she wouldn't have to finish the rest of the chili and too hungry to turn him down, she smiled. ''I'm crazy about bologna sandwiches.''

''Mustard or mayonnaise?''

''Mustard.''

''Be right back.''

Irish watched him pick up a loaf of bread from the rack and a jar of mustard off a shelf, then walk back to the meat case. He took a big sausage from the case, and she heard the whine of an electric slicing machine. In a few minutes, he returned with a neat sandwich on a piece of butcher paper. An individual bag of chips sat atop the sandwich.

''Thanks,'' she said. ''That looks great.''

''Not exactly Carnegie Deli, but it will do in a pinch. Alma Jane usually does the sandwich and soup making and helps tend to the store, but she came down with a bad case of poison ivy. I'm hoping that she'll be back tomorrow. I'm not much of a cook.''

''Me, either,'' Irish said. ''I don't even know how to work the pilot light on my stove. Olivia usually does all the cooking.''

''Who's Olivia?''

''One of my housemates in Washington.''

''One?'' He filled her glass with tea from a pitcher.

"Yes," she said. Between bites she gave him a thumbnail sketch of Olivia and Kim.

"How long have you been a reporter?" Kyle asked.

"A reporter? I'm not a reporter. Where did you get that idea?"

"You said you were doing an article on Jackson and his buddies, and I assumed that you were doing it for a newspaper."

"Heavens, no. I'm doing the article for *Esprit*."

"*Esprit*, the magazine? You work for them? I would have figured that someone with your looks would be modeling for them instead of writing."

"Thank you very much. I used to be a model." She smiled graciously. "But I don't work for the magazine full-time. This is a freelance piece."

He pointed to her uneaten bowl of chili. "Mind?"

"Not at all." His digestive tract must be lined with lead. She couldn't believe that anyone could eat an entire bowl of that blazing concoction, much less two.

"I love this stuff. It's been ages since I've had a decent bowl of chili. Grandpa Pete makes it in a wash pot over an open fire, then freezes it in bricks. Why aren't you a model any longer?"

His sudden switch of topics took her aback for a moment. She nibbled a potato chip before she gave him one of her stock answers. "I'm getting too old."

"Bull. You're gorgeous and still in your prime."

"I'm almost thirty."

He laughed. "Just a kid."

"To you maybe, but models are getting younger

and younger these days. Too, I—I was getting tired of the work, of New York.''

"Now that I can understand. The crime rate in that place is out of sight. Why, around here, the worst crime committed lately was when Newt Irwin got drunk and—Irish?''

She startled. "Pardon?''

"You flinched and looked very nervous. Did I say something? Stray into sensitive territory?''

"No. Not at all," she replied, which was a polite lie. He'd touched a nerve. "What were you saying about Luke?''

"Not Luke, Newt. He got drunk and stole one of Henry McKenzie's goats.''

"Whatever for?''

"To barbecue. But the next morning Newt's mama found the goat staked out in the front yard eating her pansies, and she called the sheriff. Henry got his goat back, but Newt had to spend three days in jail.''

"But Henry got his goat back. I'm surprised he pressed charges.''

"Henry didn't. Newt's mama did. The sheriff is married to her cousin, and Mrs. Irwin was proud of those pansies.''

Irish laughed. "Sounds like you have some real characters around here.''

A pistol shot sounded from upstairs, and Irish almost jumped out of her skin.

"That we do," Kyle said. "And one of them lives upstairs. That's Grandpa Pete again. Eighty-four years old and still rambunctious. Be right back. Look around the store and find yourself a dessert.''

Deciding to do just that, she was looking through the assortment of Twinkies, Ding-Dongs, and Little Debbie cakes when an RV stopped out front. An older couple in loud jogging gear came inside. He was balding and his jacket was stretched tightly over his rotund belly; she was rail-thin with badly colored black hair and wearing a plethora of diamond rings.

''Oh, look, Edgar. Isn't this a charming little place?'' To Irish she said, ''We're passing through on our way from the Gulf coast and decided to take the scenic route. I'm so glad we did. It's just beautiful around here, isn't it, Edgar? We wanted to pick up a few snacks, and—Edgar! Look at this. Carved Indians. Life-size. Wouldn't one of these be just precious by our pool? And look at the price. Why, it's a steal.''

''Mmmm,'' Edgar said, not glancing up from the row of snack crackers he was inspecting.

With Kyle nowhere in sight, Irish pasted on a bright smile and went into her retail mode. ''Aren't they wonderful? The sculptor is very gifted. Have you seen the animals outside? The eagles are fantastic, and there's one bear that you should see. A delightful conversation piece that was just finished. We call him Vince. Come, let me show you.''

When Kyle finally got Pete settled down and made it back downstairs, Irish was at the door waving goodbye to an RV. "Sorry I took so long, but my grand-father needed some TLC. Who was in the RV?"

"Corrie and Edgar."

"Wanting directions to Dallas?"

"Nope. They came in for snacks. I sold them a carton of soft drinks, two boxes of crackers, three jars of peanuts, two jelly rolls, two little pecan pies, two life-size Indians, an eagle and Vince. I made change for their traveler's checks from the register. I hope you don't mind."

"Mind? You sold more in thirty minutes than I've sold in a week. They bought Vince?"

"Yep."

"But his ear is missing."

"That makes him even more charming. An original."

Kyle chuckled and shook his head. "I hope that you gave them a discount."

"Certainly not. I didn't know exactly how much the bears were since none of them had a price tag, but I charged fifty dollars more than the Indian was marked."

"You're kidding?"

"Nope. Don't worry. They can afford it, and Corrie is thrilled with her new pool and garden sculptures. And quite frankly, I think they'll look cute in her back-yard. She'll have an excuse to have a party when she and Edgar get home, and the pieces are delightful conversation pieces. I told her exactly how they were made."

Kyle fought back a laugh. "Do *you* know exactly how they're made?"

Irish waved off his question. "They're carved with a chain saw. I showed them your work area and improvised some on the parts I didn't know. I told you that Corrie was thrilled."

"What about Edgar?"

"Edgar didn't say much, but he was fascinated with the rattler in the terrarium. He offered to buy the snake, but I figured it wasn't for sale. Anyway, I didn't know how much to charge or if it had been defanged."

Kyle burst into laughter. "I'm glad you didn't sell Sam. Pete would have a fit. The snake and the arrowheads are the bulk of his museum. And no, Sam hasn't been defanged."

Irish shuddered. "I'm glad that I didn't try to fish him out. They came before I got dessert. Want to split a package of chocolate cupcakes?"

"Sure." As Kyle watched Irish talk, he grew even more enchanted with her. Not only was she one hell of a gorgeous woman, but also she was a delight to be around. Animated, fun and totally unaffected, she was the antithesis of the Hollywood types that he had escaped. Given her years as a much photographed model, he was surprised by her down-to-earth behavior and forthright attitude. "You get the cupcakes, and I'll fix the coffee. How do you like yours?"

"Black for me."

In a few minutes he joined her at the table. A chocolate cupcake sat on a napkin at his place; its mate sat in front of her. "I hope you don't mind instant," he said. "The stuff in the pot was sludge."

"Instant is fine."

They ate in relative silence. When she'd finished the last bite, she licked the chocolate off her fingers and sighed. "I love junk food, especially chocolate. I had to deny myself for years. I've gained fifteen pounds since I left New York."

"They're well disguised. You seem very slender to me."

"Thanks." She grinned. "Want another cupcake?"

"Let's go for it."

She wasted no time in getting another and ripping open the package. She handed one to him and demolished the other one in a flash. After licking her fingers again, she held her mug with both hands and sipped her coffee. Her eyes glazed as she stared at a spot over his left shoulder, and a wrinkle appeared between her lovely eyebrows.

"A problem?" he asked.

"A big one. I can't go back to Washington until I...interview Jackson Crow. If he won't return until Monday, I don't have a place to stay. I was planning on being a guest at Crow's Nest." Her frown deepened. "Are those, uh, tepees outside inhabitable?"

He chuckled. "Well, the sheets and towels are clean and they don't leak, but I doubt if they're what you're used to. They're pretty basic. You would probably be more comfortable if you drove to Jacksonville or Tyler and stayed in a nicer place."

"I can't do that." Her eyes still troubled, she ran the tip of her tongue back and forth over a small area of the mug's rim. Kyle couldn't take his eyes off that bit of pink, and as he watched, mesmerized, his imagination went wild. "You see, I'm, uh, a little short on cash. I was hoping that your tepees would be cheap."

"The tepees? Cheap? Oh, they're cheap. Very cheap." Kyle almost stood up and whooped. He wasn't anxious for her to leave just yet. "As a matter of fact, your commission on the sale to Corrie and Edgar would more than cover room and board here until Jackson gets back."

Her eyes widened. "My commission?"

"Sure. And if you need a little extra cash, I could use some help around here until Alma Jane gets back tomorrow or the next day."

"Help? Doing what?"

"Tending the store while I wield the chain saw. Or better yet, how would you like reading to an irascible old man? Pete's big on reading, but his eyes play out after a while. The job wouldn't pay much, but—"

"I'll take it. But just until Jackson returns, you understand."

"Fine. We have a deal." He couldn't help the grin that spread across his face. Wonder if he could persuade Jackson to stay in Dallas a few extra days?

The wrinkle between her brows disappeared, and she beamed. "Great. If you'll give me a key, I'll get settled in."

* * *

Irish drove the Benz to the door of tepee number two and unloaded her luggage. She unlocked the door and cautiously peeked inside.

Kyle was right. It was very basic. Most of the furniture was made from bundles of twigs and sticks. There was a faded, but clean-looking, Indian blanket on the bed. The dresser was in its prime about the time of World War II, and two large paint-by-number oils were framed in rough wood and hanging on the walls. One was an Indian chief in full feather; the other, a spotted horse in a red desert. A wooden rocking chair, its seat made of taut cowhide with the hair still on, sat in a corner.

Irish sighed and hauled her things inside. "Home, sweet home."

She checked the sheets and the bed. And the locks.

The sheets were crisp and fresh-smelling, the mattress amazingly lump-free and comfortable. The bathroom fixtures were old but immaculate. And most important, the locks were sturdy. The place wasn't the Plaza, but the price was right, and it would do.

After she hung up her clothes and put her other things away, Irish changed out of her new outfit into jeans, a white T-shirt and a chambray shirt. A pair of sport shoes felt like heaven compared to the new high-heeled boots, which didn't look too bad considering the punishment they'd had. A quick repair to hair and makeup and she was ready to meet Cherokee Pete.

Sounds of the chain saw came from the shed, and Irish figured that Kyle was back at work on another bear or a bow-legged cowpoke. She went inside the store and hesitated only a moment before she tiptoed upstairs. She didn't want to disturb the old gentleman if he was still sleeping.

Following the noise of a TV, she went toward an open door off the landing, noting as she passed that the large painting on the wall there was an excellent copy of a Remington. And much more attractive than the Indian and spotted pony on her walls.

The room she peeked in was a large library. Straight ahead was a huge stone fireplace with another of the Remington copies hung on it and several Southwestern pots and such on the mantel. Two large leather couches flanked the fireplace and a coffee table, made from a slice of a huge tree, sat between the oxblood couches. Additional pots and a statue of a breech-clouted brave, much more finely wrought than the wooden ones downstairs, stood atop the table. Other wing chairs and leather club chairs with ottomans were grouped around the room. The place looked more like a gentlemen's club than the upstairs of the junky trading post below.

Floor to ceiling shelves in polished wood took up most of the available wall space, and they were filled with books. Her gaze followed the bulging shelves until they came to an alcove at one end of the room, to a hospital bed beside a window, to a pair of dark eyes watching her.

She smiled. "Hello. I'm Irish Ellison. May I come in?"

"Looks like you're in already. Come closer and let me get a good gander at you. These old eyes ain't what they used to be. Irish, you say? Never heard nobody named that except it was a nickname."

"It's my real name. My mother was mostly Irish and a romantic," she said as she crossed the room to the bed.

He reminded her of an older, more wiry version of Willie Nelson. His hair was thinning on top, but the sides hung in long gray braids. The skin over his high cheekbones was leathery and wrinkled, but his dark eyes flashed with vitality, and Irish doubted if they missed much.

He held up a remote control and pressed it. The TV sound died. "I'm Pete Beamon, but everybody calls me Cherokee Pete. Called me that as long as I can remember. Half Cherokee from my mother's side. M'wife was Irish. Honey-colored hair and blue eyes she had. Beautiful woman, like you. Been gone forty-three years next November. She was a schoolteacher. Taught me how to read after I was grown. We started collecting these books over fifty years ago. Come, sit down here." He pointed to an easy chair beside his bed. "Tell me what a pretty gal like you is doin' in these parts."

"Don't let me interrupt your—" Irish glanced to the wall where the television was and startled. Instead of a single TV, a bank of six screens were mounted there. Two were blank, but two showed the interior of the store downstairs, and two others scanned the outside grounds. "But that's—"

"Surveillance. These old eyes don't miss much. You take a hankerin' to my grandson?"

Irish cleared her throat and tried not to squirm. "He's—he's very attractive, but I'm not interested."

Cherokee Pete gave a little bark of laughter. "That's not what I saw. I like the cut of you, Irish Ellison. Could tell that right off. Tell you what. You marry my grandson, and I'll give you a million dollars."

Three

Irish laughed at the old man's joke. "He's a handsome devil. Don't tempt me. Anxious to be rid of him, are you?"

"I'm anxious to have some great-grandkids before I kick the bucket. Not a single one of my grandsons is married. Ain't natural. Kyle tells me you're going to read to me some."

"If you'd like."

"Course I'd like," Pete said. "Just cause I'm older'n dirt don't mean I can't appreciate the company of a beautiful young lady."

"What would you like for me to read?"

Pete picked up the book lying on the bed beside him and handed it to her. "I'd like to hear the rest of this. I was near 'bout finished when my eyes played out. Need new glasses, but it will be a while before I can get to the eye doctor now that I busted my hip. Kyle says he'll take me in a couple of weeks.''

Irish looked at the big volume. "John Grisham's newest. You a fan of his?"

"He's right good when I'm in the mood for his kind of book. I read purt near everything from shoot 'em ups to philosophy. My grandkids know I like readin' so I get a lots of books for Christmas and the like. Marker's where I left off.''

She opened the book at the page where the tasseled leather strip lay and started to read the last few chapters.

Kyle stood at the door and listened to Irish's beautifully modulated voice as she read to the old man. John Grisham had never sounded so exciting to him.

Or so sexy.

He didn't pay much attention to the words of the narrative, only her tone, which oozed over him like warm buttered honey. When a bit of dialogue came, she changed her voice slightly to take on the character, then switched back to the slow, sensual utterances.

At last she paused, then said, "The end.''

Grandpa Pete cackled. "A million dollars! Yes, siree, a million dollars. No. Make that *two* million.''

Irish laughed, and Kyle rushed in before his grandfather started writing out a check. Pete was very generous with people he liked. "I see that you two are getting along," Kyle said.

"Like a house afire," Pete said. "This one's a keeper. Danged if she can't make that book come alive as good as one of them New York actresses."

"I heard," Kyle said. "You are very good. Ever consider acting?"

"Early on," Irish replied. "I majored in drama for two years, but I dropped out of college and went into modeling instead."

"Modeling?" Pete asked. "I thought Kyle said you was a writer."

"I am. I don't do modeling anymore."

"Was you in the magazines like that Cindy Crawford or Claudia what's-her-name, that foreign gal?"

"Yes, but I wasn't quite in their league. How do you know about Cindy and Claudia?"

The old man winked. "Told you I read purt near everything. Even look at one of them women's magazines now and then. You know, now that I think on it, I believe I've seen your picture somewheres."

"Not for a couple of years. Would you like to start another book?"

"Not right now. I think I'll take a little nap or maybe watch Oprah. You and Kyle run along and get better acquainted." He winked meaningfully at Irish again. "If you know what I mean."

She laughed. "Not on your life."

As Irish and Kyle walked downstairs, he asked,

"What is my grandfather up to now? He hasn't made any indecent proposals has he?"

"No. We were just joking. He offered me a million dollars if I would marry you. Then he upped it to two."

"My God!"

"Don't worry. I didn't take him seriously. I know that the proceeds from this place and his monthly Social Security check haven't made him a millionaire, but he's an old dear anyway. If he were rolling in dough though, I might have to give his offer serious consideration."

Kyle's step faltered. "Oh?"

She smiled. "I'm sure that I'm not the first woman to tell you that you're an extremely attractive man. And two million dollars would make you darned near irresistible."

His step faltered again. "Money turn you on?"

"Green is my very favorite color. As I said, you're an attractive guy in lots of ways, but you're safe from me. No offense intended, but I plan on marrying a rich man."

All sorts of alarms started going off in his head. "That so?"

"Yep."

"What about love?"

"Oh, I don't want just any rich man. I want one that I can love, of course. But being able to sleep soundly without worrying about security generates a lot of affection."

Her tone was light and teasing, but Kyle sensed an underlying agenda that prompted her attitude. What was it that worried her at night? He wondered if it had anything to do with the scars on the left side of her face. The faint lines were almost imperceptible. With her skillful makeup, nobody but a professional giving her as close a scrutiny as he had would have detected the slight traces.

He ached to ask her more, but now was not the time. Instead he chuckled and said, "I'll drink to that. Do you mind watching the store for a while? I need to check some things with my grandfather."

"No problem."

He turned and hurried back upstairs.

When Pete spied Kyle, he said, "What are you doing up here? Why ain't you down courtin' Irish? I like her, son. I like her a lot. She'd make you a fine wife. You'd have good-looking kids."

"Aren't you rushing things a bit?"

"Nope. I knew right off that your grandmother was the woman for me."

"Well, I'm different," Kyle said. "I need a bit more time. And there's a hitch with Irish."

"A hitch?"

Kyle sat down beside the bed and blew out a big breath. "It seems that she wants to marry a rich man."

Pete gave a hoot of laughter. "Then you're in good shape there. Besides the ten I gave you, how many million did you have at last count?"

"That's not the point. You see, I could be very in-

terested in Irish, but I don't want somebody who looks
at me and only sees dollar signs."

Pete nodded. "I get you. So you're going to lie to
her?"

"No. Yes." Kyle dropped his hat on his knee and
ran his fingers through his hair. "Hell, I don't know.
But I wouldn't want to fall for a gold digger. For the
moment I'd just as soon that she not know that you're
wealthy or that I'm wealthy or—"

"Or that you're a plastic surgeon."

"Right. Or that Jackson is your grandson and my
cousin."

"Why is that?"

Kyle grinned. "Because I'm going to see if I can
stall Jackson and that bunch of his in Dallas for an
extra day or two. I don't want Irish tempted by all
those men and all that money until I can get a toehold
in her affections."

"Won't she suspect something if she sees the oil
wells on the property?"

"If she mentions it, I'll tell her that they belong to
Jackson or somebody. She won't have any way of
knowing that the land is yours. Will you play along
with me?"

"My lips are sealed. As far as I'm concerned,
you're nothing but a shiftless bum, and I'm one step
away from food stamps."

"You don't have to go quite *that* far."

Cherokee Pete's eyes twinkled. "I do believe

you've taken quite a liking to our Irish already for you to go to so much trouble.''

"I'll admit that she intrigues me.''

Pete cackled. "*Intrigues,* hell. She's got your juices pumping. I ain't so old I can't remember. Check that roast you put in the oven, then go on down there and get to courtin'.''

Kyle decided to do just that.

He and Irish spent the rest of the afternoon in the store, waiting on the occasional customer and talking about everything from favorite colors to politics. They found that, despite a difference in their backgrounds and the fact that he liked blue to her green, they had a lot in common. In fact, after gazing for a spell into those lovely emerald green eyes of hers, he was beginning to change his mind about blue. Green was enchanting.

At dinnertime, They went upstairs and Kyle checked the roast that he had prepared earlier under Pete's tutelage. He poked the meat with a fork, then poked the carrots, onions and potatoes. "That looks done to me. Does it look done to you?''

"I'm no expert, but it seems to be.''

"We'll declare it done. Want a salad?''

"Sure,'' she said. "I can make salad.''

They both pitched in to chop the vegetables, and Irish prepared a tray for Pete. While she took the tray to his grandfather, Kyle set the kitchen table for them. He started to put a candle in the middle, then decided that was pushing it a bit. He dug around until he found a cheap jug of burgundy and an expensive bottle of chardonnay. He put the chardonnay in the refrigerator and unscrewed the cap on the burgundy.

Irish returned as he was taking glasses from the cabinet. The Baccarat crystal stems that Kyle had given his grandfather on his last birthday were next to the jelly glasses. Kyle smiled, shook his head and poured a little from the jug to taste.

"Not bad for the price," Kyle said. "Grandpa Pete isn't much of a wine connoisseur. Will this do?"

"Sure. I'm not too fussy myself. Truthfully, some of the stuff that's supposed to be so fine tastes like medicine to me."

After dinner they cleaned up the kitchen together and got Pete settled down watching a John Wayne movie on cable.

"I guess that I'd better mosey on back to my tepee," Irish said, smiling. "Thanks for dinner."

"My pleasure. Want to take a walk first?"

"Sure."

Outside the evening was still pleasantly warm, even though it was October. The air carried the crisp smell of pine trees and the watermelon scent of fresh cut grass. In the gathering darkness, crickets and tree frogs tuned up. Irish had noticed earlier that everything was still green; even the hardwood trees mixed in with the pines showed no signs of fall. She commented that the weather surprised her. "When does it get cool here? When do the leaves change?"

"Depends on what you call cool. Brief fronts begin pushing through beginning about now. The temperature will drop a few degrees, then warm up again in a day or two. We rarely get a frost before November, sometimes later than that. The leaves start turning about then, too, but because of the weather and because we have so many pines, autumn here is nothing like New England. A few trees are colorful—sweetgums, tallows, some elms and oaks. Most of the others that lose their leaves stay green until frost, then turn brown and shed in November or December. By March they're leafing out again."

Because of darkness outside the range of the tall vapor lights, they didn't wander far from the trading post and their walk was more amble than exercise.

As they strolled by the shed, Irish said, "I see that you've started a new bear." She stepped inside where the strong odor of fresh sawdust and wood shavings scented the air. She rubbed her thumbs over the rough-cut ears of the bear that stood as tall as she. "I felt so terrible about making you ruin the other one that I was relieved when Corrie bought it."

"Nothing for you to feel terrible about. It was an accident."

"Is this what you did in California, carve bears?"

"No. I, uh, did a different kind of sculpting."

"What kind? Clay?"

Kyle gave her a vague answer, and she gathered that he wasn't comfortable talking about his time on the West Coast. She could understand that; she wasn't too comfortable talking about the last couple of years she spent in New York.

He ducked and entered the shed to stand beside her. The space suddenly became smaller, the raw wood smell more pungent. One of his thumbs traced a path over the bear's ear, a path that was parallel to the course her thumb took and only a millimeter away from touching hers.

The space grew smaller still. His scent mingled with the woody aroma and his closeness bombarded her senses until his presence loomed larger than life and seemed to crackle and glow in her awareness.

Jerking her thumb back, she tried to step away from him, but she bumped against the bear's outstretched paw. Finding herself penned between the bear's paws and Kyle, she glanced up, her mouth open to deliver a clever quip.

The words vanished from her mind.

He hesitated for a moment, then slowly his head lowered. "May I kiss you?" he asked as his lips came closer and closer. They stopped when they were a hairsbreadth from hers.

Her heart began racing, and his breath against her skin sent tingles of excitement over her. A part of her wanted to shout, "Yes!" Another part wanted to smack him for putting her in such a bind and growl, "No!"

But she was mute. Neither word would form on her lips.

For an eon, they stood there. The air around them hummed with sensual awareness.

Her knees twitched.

Her ears roared.

Don't do this, a rational part of her brain whispered.

Get lost, her libido replied.

Yes was winning.

She moistened her lips and was about to close the tiny gap when a loud pistol shot cracked the quiet.

Four

Just after dawn the ruckus started. A horn blared outside Irish's door and something bashed into her wall hard enough to rattle the pictures.

"What the—" She sat straight up in bed. Another horn blasted through the fog in her brain, and she heard loud voices and car doors slamming.

Throwing back the covers, she hurried to the window and peeked out. It looked as if the gypsies had invaded while she slept. Tents were everywhere. Tents and blue canopies and long tables under trees. There must have been thirty or more trucks and cars with trailers scattered around outside the trading post. People were unloading all sorts of stuff from furniture to vegetables.

A wooden trailer that advertised snow cones, popcorn and cotton candy for sale was butted up against her tepee, and a man was waving his arms and shouting, trying to direct the driver of the pickup pulling it.

The trailer pulled forward, then backed up again. *Whomp!* It slammed against the side of the tepee.

Irish rushed to the door, shoved aside the chest she'd dragged across it to block the way, turned the lock and threw the bolt. "What are you *doing?*" she yelled. "Trying to demolish the place while I sleep?"

The florid-faced fellow doing the directing stopped waving and gawked at her. Then he swept off his cowboy hat and dropped his eyes. "Sorry, ma'am. Jason can't quite get the hang of it."

"Get the hang of what?"

"Parkin' the stand in the right place."

The truck door opened and a dejected carrot-topped boy, who couldn't have been more than fourteen, climbed out. "I can't do it, Daddy."

"Well, you're gonna have to. Your mama ain't here to do it."

"But, Daddy—"

"Shut your mouth and get back in that truck before I take a strap to you."

"Over my dead body!" Irish stormed. She strode to the truck. "Where do you want this thing?"

When the man described the placement he was after, Irish said, "Get in, Jason. I'll help you."

Jason, his eyes as big as saucers, got in the truck. Irish climbed on the running board and very quietly

directed the boy until they slowly maneuvered the
stand into place.

"There you go," she said. "Perfect."

A wide grin spread over the boy's face.

When she stepped off the running board, she realized that all the activity nearby had stopped and people
were staring. That's when it dawned on her that she
was barefoot and wearing only a satin sleep-shirt. A
very revealing satin sleep-shirt.

Irish didn't let it phase her. She'd posed for cata-
logue ads with less on. Nose in the air, she marched
into her tepee and slammed the door.

She looked at the clock and groaned. Who got up
at such an ungodly hour? Wanting nothing so much
as to climb back between the sheets, she conceded that
trying to get any more sleep was a lost cause and
headed for the shower. She hadn't slept worth a darn.
Even though the bed was comfortable, she'd tossed
and turned for hours before she'd finally drifted off.

Kyle Rutledge had been the cause of her restless
night. She couldn't believe that she had allowed him
to get under her skin so. If old Pete hadn't fired his
pistol at the right time, in another moment she and
Kyle would have been locked in a steamy kiss—and
God knows what else might have happened.

She found Kyle *much* too appealing, and he wasn't
the kind of man that she was interested in, she kept
telling herself. He was poor; she wanted rich. If she
had any other options, she would leave this place and
remove herself from temptation.

Because Kyle Rutledge was very, very tempting.

But, with her financial situation, she had no other options.

She dressed quickly in jeans and an old favorite jersey, took her time with her ritual makeup job and went in search of breakfast.

If the outside looked like an anthill, inside the trading post was even more chaotic. Both tables were full with people drinking coffee and eating rolls and doughnuts, and about a dozen others milled around the store. Kyle stood behind the counter looking harried.

Irish joined him. "You look as if you could use some help."

"You bet I could. I forgot that this was third Saturday. It's trading day—a big deal around here. People come from miles away to buy, sell, or swap."

"What can I do?"

"Make another pot of coffee, help customers, mind the register, cut up a dozen chickens—"

"A *dozen* chickens?"

"Maybe more. I don't know. They were supposed to be already cut up, but they delivered whole ones instead. Grandpa Pete always has fried chicken, baked potatoes and coleslaw to sell to the lunch crowd. Alma Jane promised to come, poison ivy and all, and fry the chicken, but I have to cut it up first. Truthfully, I don't remember ever dissecting one of the blasted things."

"You make the coffee, and I'll start on the chickens."

"You know how? I thought you couldn't cook."

"I'm not much on cooking, but my father was a butcher. I worked in the shop after school and on Saturdays." She picked up a white apron and put it on. "All you need is a sharp knife and a strong stomach. Where are the knives?"

Between making pots of coffee, waiting on customers and wrapping potatoes to bake, Kyle watched Irish handle the knife like a pro. The large bowls of chicken pieces grew as she tossed light meat into one, dark into another and bony parts into a third.

"Your speed amazes me," he said.

"Me too. I haven't done this in years, but it's like riding a bike. After a few minutes it all came back to me, and I went on automatic." She tossed the last parts into a bowl and turned to him. "Ta, ta! All done." Smiling, she held the knife aloft like a prize.

Chuckling, he said, "I'm impressed. Honey, the way you wield that knife, I wouldn't want to meet you alone in a dark alley."

Her smile died. Her face paled. She looked at the knife in her hand as if it were a rattlesnake, then flung it aside and ran toward the door.

Kyle didn't have the vaguest notion what had upset her, but she was unquestionably seriously disturbed. He dropped what he was doing and hurried after her.

When he found her, she was down at the far end of the porch, her arms wrapped around one of the large support timbers, and gulping deep breaths of air.

"Irish, what's wrong?"

She shook her head, averted her face and continued her deep breathing. "Give me a minute."

"Are you ill?"

She shook her head again. "I'll be okay. Just leave me alone for a little while."

"I'm not going anywhere with you like this."

"*Please.* Go away, dammit!"

Since his presence seemed to agitate her more, Kyle had no choice but to leave. But he was troubled by her behavior. Had cutting up those chickens made her nauseous? She'd said something about needing a strong stomach. Damn! Why had he let her do it? He felt like a first-class jerk.

When he returned to the store, he didn't have time to worry anymore. Customers were four deep at the counter. While he was ringing up sales, Alma Jane arrived carrying a huge container of coleslaw. He could have kissed the tall, raw-boned woman, lotion-covered spots and all.

"Mornin'," she said with a curt nod of her head.

"Good morning, Alma Jane. I've never been so glad to see anybody in my life. I really appreciate your coming to work today."

She nodded again. "Chicken cut up?"

"Right there."

She pulled on a long pair of rubber gloves over her swollen, rash-reddened hands and inspected the parts in the bowls. "Good job."

"You can thank Irish for that."

"Who's Irish?"

He glanced toward the door and smiled. "Here she comes now."

"Fine-looking woman."

His smile broadened. "That she is." Irish still looked a little wobbly, but she was all smiles and graciousness when he introduced her to Alma Jane. "Are you all right?" he asked her quietly.

"I'm fine." Her clipped answer announced clearly that she didn't want to discuss the incident. "Has Pete had his breakfast yet?"

Kyle slapped his head. "God, I got so busy here, I forgot all about Pete. I hope he hasn't gotten out of bed. He's only supposed to use his walker to get to the bathroom."

"I'll take coffee up and check on him." She drew two mugs from the big urn and went upstairs.

He watched her go, still concerned about her.

"Kyle Rutledge, quit moonin' over that woman and get to work," Alma Jane said.

Kyle laughed and kissed her cheek. "Now, Alma Jane, you know I don't hanker after any woman except you."

"Oh, go on with you, you smooth-tongued devil. I'll not have my head turned with any of your sweet talk. Finish wrapping them potatoes for the oven or they'll never be done."

"Yes, ma'am."

Irish prepared scrambled eggs and toast for Pete's breakfast, sat beside his bed and ate some along with him.

"Good crowd today?" he asked as he spread jelly on a slice of his toast.

"Looks like it, but I don't know how many you usually have. Things are busy downstairs. Alma Jane is frying chicken and Kyle is handling the register." She scooped a last bite of egg into her mouth. "I probably need to go help them. Or shall I read to you for a while?"

"You run along. I'll let you know if I need anything." He chuckled and patted the pistol laying on his bedside table.

"Wouldn't a bell be better?"

"Nope. Hard to hear a bell at any distance. Damned near impossible if Kyle is running the chain saw. Can't miss Suzi here."

"Makes sense to me. I'll bring you up some chicken later."

Irish went back down to the store and got busy, stopping only to take a plate to Pete at lunchtime. Alma Jane's rash was bothering her, and she left as soon as all the chicken was fried and in the warming bin and a big pot of soup made from the bony pieces was simmering on the stove. Both Irish and Kyle kept on the move dishing food onto paper plates, bussing tables, ringing up sales and answering questions. By the time the crowd started thinning out late that afternoon, they were both exhausted.

Kyle poured two glasses of iced tea, handed one to

Irish and led her to one of the tables. "I'm declaring a break. I don't think I ever want to see another bologna sandwich or plate of fried chicken." He sat down and propped his feet on an empty chair. "I don't see how Grandpa Pete handles this at his age."

Grateful to sit down, Irish took a big swallow of tea and sighed. "Me, either. I'm over fifty years younger than he is, and I'm pooped. This is worse than freebie day at the makeup counter."

"The makeup counter?"

"My day job. I sell special cosmetics at a department store in D.C."

"Special in what way?"

"It's a makeup base that covers scars and birthmarks without looking as if it were applied with a putty knife. See, I wear it." She angled the left side of her face toward him.

"You have a birthmark?"

"No. I have scars. From a knife. They're really almost gone now. I had an excellent plastic surgeon."

Kyle was quiet for a moment. "You must have had a very difficult time. Want to talk about it?"

She drew a deep breath. "Not now. Oh, there's a customer. Keep your seat. I'll take care of him."

Quickly she rose and went behind the register. Funny, just about the time that she was sure that she was past all the fallout from her horrifying encounter, something cropped up to prove that she wasn't completely over it after all. At least she didn't have the nightmares anymore. Two years of therapy had resolved that problem.

About sundown, when the sellers and traders had marked down their remaining merchandise to rock-bottom prices, Irish took a break to stroll through the stalls and tables. She waved at Jason, who was tending the cotton candy machine, and he waved back, then ducked his head quickly.

Even the picked-over stuff was interesting. The vendors had everything from homemade jellies and relishes to antiques to junk. With her resources so low, she couldn't do much more than look. Since there was no TV in her tepee, she did spring for three used paperback novels that went for a quarter.

As she turned away from making her purchase, she found Jason standing behind her holding a cone of cotton candy. He thrust it out to her. "This is for you, ma'am."

She smiled brightly. "Aren't you a sweetheart? I adore cotton candy."

The boy turned several shades pinker than the confection, turned, and fled.

Irish heard a soft laugh and glanced over her shoulder. Kyle stood there. "I believe you have another admirer."

"Another?"

"Besides me and every other male over puberty on the place."

A toddler ran squealing toward them, and the curly-haired little boy wrapped his arms around one of Irish's legs. She handed the cotton candy to Kyle and picked up the child who was dressed in grass-stained red-and-yellow striped overalls with a red knit shirt. "Hi, there. Aren't you a cutie?"

He stuck his finger in his mouth, and his drooling grin showed four newly emerging baby teeth.

"I'll have to adjust that age limit downward," Kyle said. "Looks like you've stolen another heart."

"With a slightly damp bottom. Where's your mommy, cutie-pie?"

"Ma-ma," the child said, throwing his arms around her neck and squeezing.

Irish almost melted into a puddle. She'd never realized how adorable babies could be. Especially ones who called her Mama. She patted and rubbed his back while he clung to her like a little monkey. "Do you suppose he's lost?"

"I'm sure his mother is around somewhere and just hasn't missed him yet," Kyle said. "Let's walk around and look for her. Here, let me carry him."

The toddler would have none of that. He hung on to Irish's neck for dear life. "Ma-ma. Ma-ma," he cried as Kyle tried to pry him away.

"Shhhh, sweetie," she soothed, patting his back. "I'd better carry him. He's not very heavy. Who's minding the store?"

"Jenny, a neighbor from down the road said that she'd take over for a few minutes. She helps out sometimes, but she was in Tyler earlier today. Someone from her church was in the hospital.''

The vendors were packing to leave as Irish and Kyle walked around the grounds questioning everyone they met. Nobody had lost a child.

They walked back to the store where Kyle relieved Jenny and locked the register. In the gathering dusk, they stood on the porch and watched the trucks and vans depart one by one. The last to leave were Jason and his father. She waved to Jason as the trailer pulled away.

"Bye-bye," the child in her arms said, waving as well.

"We have a problem," Irish said.

"I know. Maybe I'd better call the sheriff."

"Good idea. But first, does the store carry diapers?"

"I think so. The disposable kind."

"Do you know how to change diapers?" she asked.

"Piece of cake."

Five minutes later the toddler was laid out on a segment of butcher paper covering one of the tables. Kyle had gathered up a box of disposable wipes, baby powder and a package of diapers. In no time at all, he had removed the old sodden diaper, cleaned, powdered and changed the child.

"I'm impressed," Irish said as she watched him efficiently smooth the tapes into place.

"I baby-sit with my godson sometimes. He's just a few months old, but the principle is the same. There you go, tiger." He snapped the overalls into place and picked up the little boy.

As soon as the child spotted Irish, he held out his arms to her. "Ma-ma. Ba-ba."

She took him. "I'm not your mama, sweetie, but we'll find her soon."

He patted her cheeks with his chubby hands and said, "Ba-ba. Num. Ba-ba. Num."

"Ba-ba num to you, too, cutie-pie." She rubbed her nose against his little snubbed one.

He patted her cheeks harder. "Ba-ba! Num!"

"I don't have a clue as to what he wants," she said to Kyle. "Do you?"

"Unless he's hungry."

"Of course! Ba-ba is bottle. You want a bottle, pumpkin?"

The toddler jumped up and down in her arms. "Ba-ba!"

She looked at Kyle out of the corner of her eye. "Uh, I hope you have some bottles and some milk around."

"Milk, yes. Bottles? I'm not sure. But we carry baby food. And I think that there's a high chair in the storage room. Let me check on Pete quickly, then I'll get it."

A few minutes later, the child was settled in a high chair and had a kitchen towel tied around his neck for a bib. He drank some milk from a paper cup and, even with Irish holding it firmly, in his exuberance he managed to slop a good portion of his milk onto the tray of the high chair and the rest of it on the floor.

He laughed and slapped his hands in the resulting mess as Irish tried to feed him strained carrots, peas and chicken. Kyle tried to clean up the spills.

"He doesn't seem too fond of peas," Kyle said as the child spit out the third spoonful of them and the green goo dribbled down his chin.

"No, but he loves carrots. Yum-yum," she said, feeding him another bite of the orange puree.

"Num," he said in return.

"Now we know what 'num' means," Kyle said.

"Num-num!" The child banged on the tray and opened his mouth like a bird for more. In no time, he polished off the carrots, chicken, a jar of applesauce and another cup of milk.

"The kid has an appetite." Kyle washed tiny fingers and a stained mouth with a damp paper towel. "I guess I'd better call the sheriff now."

The toddler held out his arms to Irish. "Up, Mama. Up."

"Oh, you sweet thing, how could anybody go off and leave you?" She lifted the little one from the chair and snuggled him against her while Kyle made his phone call. When Kyle returned, she said, "When is he coming?"

"I don't know. The dispatcher said that they have an emergency situation and that every person is tied up and will be for hours."

There was a loud banging on the front door, and Kyle went to unlock it.

A small blond woman, wild-eyed and sobbing, stood there. "My baby, I've lost my—" When she spotted the toddler, she screamed, "Joey!" and charged toward Irish and the child.

"Ma-ma!" Joey squirmed and held out his arms.

The woman grabbed him, hugged him fiercely and rained dozens of kisses on his face. "Oh, thank God! Thank God! I've been frantic. He was asleep in the back seat and his older sisters were supposed to be watching him, but they got distracted. I was only gone a few minutes to buy some vegetables, but he must have slipped out of the car when they were looking at the puppies. I thought he was still asleep, and I drove almost to Wills Point before I discovered he was missing. Oh, Joey, baby." She covered his chubby cheeks with more kisses.

The mother was profuse in her thanks and offered Irish and Kyle a reward for finding her son. They politely refused.

When she and the child left, Irish and Kyle stood on the porch of the trading post waving goodbye. Their arms automatically went around each others waists, and she laid her head on his shoulder.

"It's amazing how the little buggers can burrow into your heart so quickly," he said.

She nodded. "He was so adorable."

"Ever think about having kids of your own?" His

hand that had rested on her hipbone moved slowly, stroking toward her tummy.

His touch sent little shivers over her, but she struggled to keep her voice calm. "Occasionally, but only in a vague sort of way. I really haven't been around children very much."

"You would make a good mother." He kissed her forehead.

She smiled and looked up at him. "I need to find a husband first."

He leaned against the railing and pulled her to him. "Are you looking?"

In the dim light his eyes shone like blue flames as his mouth lowered toward hers. As if mesmerized by his gaze, she lifted her face. "Yes."

His lips touched hers tentatively. She knew that he was giving her the opportunity to pull away, but she couldn't seem to remember how to make her muscles move. The masculine scent that clung to him, the virile male aura that vibrated around him had fogged her reason and jammed her good judgment frequencies.

His lips were soft. And warm. And wonderful.

And oh, so sexy.

"Yes," she whispered again, forgetting the question. Her arms slid around him; her lips parted.

His mouth covered hers, and the earth moved.

Firecrackers exploded in every cell in her body. Sparklers sizzled and spewed over her skin. His tongue plunged deeply, and Roman candles went off in her head.

Frightened by her reaction, she quickly pulled back, but her knees were too wobbly to move. She dropped her head against his chest and tried to catch her breath. "Oh, dear," she said, sucking in a ragged lungful of air. She wasn't supposed to let this happen. He was all wrong. Not at all the sort of man she wanted.

"What kind of man are you looking for?" he asked, as if he could read her mind. His hands roamed over her back, making long strokes down to the swell of her bottom.

Her derriere started to quiver like aspic in an earthquake. She couldn't let this continue! She tightened her muscles and her resolve.

"I told you before. A rich one." Her voice sounded funny, kind of squeaky. "And I don't plan to get involved with someone like you, no offense intended."

"I see." Damned if he didn't lift her chin and kiss her again.

Cherry bombs and skyrockets. A whole Fourth of July display lit the sky of her sensual awareness. She couldn't allow him to keep on kissing her like that. She was going to stop him in a minute.

In just one minute.

Grabbing handfuls of his wonderful thick hair, she meant to yank his head back and his lips from hers, but somehow the signals to her fingers got scrambled. She pulled him closer instead, sighing against his hungry mouth and pressing her breasts to his chest.

She would stop him in just one minute.

Or maybe two.

When he finally dragged his mouth from hers, she whimpered.

"Dear God," he groaned, his breath ragged.

Her breathing wasn't any better. She sounded as if she were having an asthma attack. "You're not my type," she told him emphatically.

"Right." He kissed her again.

Five

Kyle slammed down the kitchen phone and cursed. Where the hell was Jackson anyhow? He had called his cousin's Dallas hotel suite half a dozen times in the past two days and hadn't been able to reach him. Damn!

"Problems?"

He glanced up to find Irish standing in the doorway. Had she overheard him leaving a message for Jackson? God, he hoped not. He was sunk if she had. "Excuse me?"

She grinned. "I heard you commenting negatively on someone's parentage, and you sounded annoyed. I asked if you were having problems."

"Not really. I was trying to reach a friend of mine,

and he wasn't home. Did Grandpa Pete eat all his breakfast?''

"Every bite. I offered to read to him, but he told me to run along. He said that he wanted to watch church services on TV."

"*Church services?* Grandpa Pete?"

"That's what he said. Want some frozen waffles?"

"I prefer mine warm."

Irish chuckled. "I may not be much of a cook, but I can work a toaster just fine." She opened the freezer and took out a package.

While she toasted waffles, he set the kitchen table and poured orange juice. Just as he refilled their coffee mugs, she put their plates on the table.

"We're a great team," he said.

She didn't comment.

"Yes, sir, a great team. Our timing is excellent. Don't you think so?" he asked, holding her chair.

She sat down, slathered her waffles in butter and drizzled syrup over them before she commented. Even then, she appeared to choose her words very carefully before she spoke. "Kyle, we seem to work very well together—in the kitchen and in the trading post, but…well, that kiss last night shouldn't have happened. It wouldn't have happened if we hadn't been so caught up in the emotion of the moment, finding Joey and then having his mother show up, I mean. That's all it was, a spontaneous response to a tender, shared experience."

"You think so?" He could tell that she was struggling to make a point, and he tried to keep the amusement from his voice. He hadn't heard so much gobbledygook since the last political rally he'd attended.

"I know so. Now I've told you that I find you attractive, but I'm not about to get involved with you. You're a very nice man, and I'd like very much for us to be friends, but we can never be anything more than that."

"Because you're looking for a rich man?"

"Right. I know that may sound mercenary to you, but that's the way that it is, and I want to be very clear. That kiss was just...just—"

"A spontaneous reaction to the emotion of the moment." Not making eye contact with her, Kyle casually doused his waffles with syrup.

"Right. It meant nothing." Irish carefully cut and ate a bite.

"I understand. And if it should happen again, I shouldn't assume that it's anything more than another spontaneous reaction between friends."

"Exactly." Her head jerked up. "No! I mean, it's not going to happen again."

"Because we're only friends."

"Right."

"Friends. And there's no sexual chemistry between us."

"Right."

He couldn't help the little snort of a laugh from escaping.

Her eyes narrowed. "What was that for?"

Kyle composed his face into a mask of innocence. "What was what for?"

"That sound you made."

"Must be my allergies acting up again. Say, how would you like to drive over to Tyler with me this afternoon? I have to pick up some things, and Jenny is coming to tend to the store and look in on Pete. She'll be here as soon as church is over. We could have a late lunch and maybe go to a movie. My treat. How does that sound?"

"Sounds great. How far away is Tyler?"

"Only about thirty-five or forty miles from here. I'm sure you passed through on your way from Dallas."

They finished their breakfast in silence, but Kyle could almost hear her thoughts chattering as loudly as his were. No sexual chemistry between them, indeed. Any more chemistry and the whole place would go up in a mushroom cloud. Even being in the same room with Irish made the ethers hum. In another few days he could convince her that they truly would be perfect together.

If only he could head off Jackson and delay his return.

Irish wished Jackson would hurry back to Crow's Nest. She needed to get away from Kyle Rutledge before she did something foolish. Touching perfume behind her ears, she told herself that even going to Tyler with Kyle was playing with fire. She was surprised that her nose wasn't two feet long from saying that there was no sexual chemistry between them. She had lied big time.

Finally satisfied with her carefully selected neutral outfit—beige slacks and silk shirt—she added gold chains and hoop earrings, then grabbed a string purse and went to meet Kyle.

He was waiting on the porch. And from the way his eyes devoured her, her plan to downplay her appearance was a dismal failure. She might as well have been wearing a black lace teddy.

He smiled in a blatantly provocative way. "You look lovely."

"Thank you." She bit back the urge to say that he wasn't exactly a slouch himself. Unless she was badly mistaken, the cut of his dark slacks and ecru shirt were Italian. Expensive, designer Italian that screamed West Coast chic. Even if his outfit was a rip-off or bought at a resale shop, it hadn't been cheap. No wonder he hadn't succeeded in California. He must have spent all his money on clothes.

"Jenny just arrived, and we can leave if you're ready."

"I'm ready."

He escorted her to a bright blue pickup parked in front. "Hope you don't mind riding in Pete's truck. I have to pick up some supplies."

"I don't mind at all. I can't remember ever riding in one before."

"You're kidding."

"Nope. I'm afraid my education is sadly lacking." When she noticed the logo on the truck door, Irish raised an eyebrow. Inside a circle was a cartoonlike Native American wearing braids and a feather, and outside the arcs, Cherokee Pete's Trading Post was emblazoned in twig letters. "With today's concern about being politically correct, I'm surprised that Pete would have this on his truck."

Kyle laughed. "My grandfather isn't into being politically correct. To put it mildly, at his age he finds it confusing, but he expresses his feelings on the situation much more colorfully. None of this Native American stuff for him. His mother was an Indian and he's an Indian. Or actually, he's only half Cherokee. The other half is plain Anglo-Saxon."

"So that makes you..."

"One-eighth Cherokee, seven-eights hodgepodge, mostly English, Irish and Swedish, with a some French thrown in somewhere. What kind of food do you like? I've been itching for some Italian or Chinese myself."

As it turned out, they had both. For lunch they had pasta at a great Italian restaurant and brought Chinese takeout home to share with Pete. In between they went to a movie, then picked up several cartons of paper goods from a warehouse.

Irish wished she could have said that she didn't particularly enjoy herself, but she did. Kyle may not have been husband material, but he was great fun. He was both a gentleman of the old school and a very with-it nineties guy. She felt...cherished, charmed and thoroughly entertained.

Kyle was considerate, a wonderful conversationalist, and oozed animal magnetism. He was so darned handsome that women turned to gape and elbow other women companions, but he seemed not to notice their attention. His focus was totally on her, and he had only to brush her arm or sweep her with one of those slow, sexy looks of his to make her want to jump his bones. The man was darned near perfect.

Too bad he was poor.

She had to remind herself over and over that she was hunting for bigger game. And that's exactly what she told Kyle when he tried to kiss her again that night—the second time. Or was it the third? He'd caught her off guard at first, but after a few minutes she'd gathered her wits and pushed him away.

"I—I'll be leaving tomorrow," she said.

"Leaving?"

"Jackson Crow should be back by tomorrow, don't you think? And after all, he's the reason that I'm here. For the magazine article, I mean." She squinched up her shoulders. "Don't do that!"

"Do what?"

"Nibble my neck."

"Was I nibbling?" He ran his tongue around the rim of her ear and nipped her lobe. "Didn't you like it? I thought from all those moaning noises you were making that you liked it."

"I was *not* moaning!"

"Sorry, my mistake. It sounded like moaning to me."

"It wasn't. And get your tongue out of my ear and your hand off my breast."

He brushed her nipple with his thumb. It went rock hard instantly. "You don't like that, either?"

"Absolutely not."

"Funny, you were making that little noise again— the one that sounds like moaning but isn't."

"You need to clean out your ears. Get away from me!"

"I can't, darlin'."

"Why not?"

"Because you're holding me too tight."

She tried to move her arms. She really did. "I think I'm paralyzed," she whispered before she raised her lips to his. Just one more kiss, she told herself. One for the road.

When they finally parted, she locked and bolted the door, then leaned back against the rough wood for the longest time, savoring the lingering sensation of his lips on hers. Too bad he was poor.

But he was, and that was that.

She dragged the heavy chest across the door and double-checked all the windows to make sure that they were locked and the sturdy metal poles she always carried with her were wedged tightly against the sash.

The next morning Alma Jane marched in and announced that she was returning to work. Her poison ivy rash had become "tolerable" she said. Kyle was out in the shed working on a new design with the chain saw, and Irish had just finished reading a chapter of Warren Buffet's latest investment book to Pete.

"This seems a strange choice after Grisham and Clancy," she said to the old man. "I've never even heard of Buffet before. Don't you find this stuff boring?"

"Nope. I like to keep up with Warren's doings. He's a smart man. Paying attention to him has made me—" He stopped abruptly and coughed.

"Made you what?"

"Made me think of ways to invest my pension. Not that I have much to invest, you understand. Listen, you hear that?"

"Hear what?"

"Oh, I forgot. Er, nothing. I didn't hear nothing. How 'bout we watch a little of 'The Price is Right'? I'm right fond of Bob Barker." He punched on the TV and turned the volume to an earsplitting level.

"Pete! That's too loud." Irish grabbed the remote control and muted the sound. That's when she clearly heard the distinctive clatter of rotors overhead. She ran to the window and looked out. "It's a helicopter. A big black-and-white one. And it's almost skimming the treetops."

"Danged fool! He's gonna kill hisself one of these days."

"Who is it?"

"Er, uh, well, I don't rightly know."

"Look! There's another helicopter headed the same way. Jackson Crow must have returned. I'd better go pack."

"Pack? What for? I thought you took a shine to staying here with us. Who's gonna read to me if you take off?"

"Oh, Pete, I'm sorry." She kissed the old man's brow as he lay pouting like a child. "You understood that this was only temporary. I have a job to do."

"Writin' about that bunch of scalawags? A waste of good paper if'n you ask me."

She smiled at his pique. "I take it that you don't approve of Jackson Crow and the members of the young millionaires' club."

"Ain't that I approve or disapprove. Just seems to me that the whole lot of them ought to settle down and find themselves wives and start raising families instead of gallivanting around in helicopters or knocking little white balls around the old cornfields. Especially Jackson."

Irish chuckled. "Tell you what, I'll do my best to take at least one of them out of circulation. How about that?"

He frowned. "One of *them?* I thought you was gettin' sorta sweet on Kyle."

"Your grandson is a very nice man, Pete, but my intentions haven't changed. Kyle and I are only friends." Irish kissed his forehead again. "I hope that your appointment with the doctor today goes well. I'll come and visit you in a day or two."

Unexpected tears constricted her throat as she left Pete's room and went down the front steps of the trading post.

She didn't stop by the shed to speak with Kyle. Telling herself that she didn't want to interrupt his work, she hurried toward her tepee to dress and pack. As her hand touched the doorknob, she heard a gunshot behind her.

Six

The gate was open this time. She followed a delivery truck down the narrow lane to Crow's Nest.

The lodge, multileveled and built of rock and weathered wood with lots of glass, followed the contours of the hill where it stood and blended perfectly with the pine and hardwood forest around it. But there was nothing quaint about the place. It was huge. And it reeked of money and class.

As she pulled to a stop in front, Irish could see other, smaller cabins scattered among the trees and connected by winding rock walkways. Opposite the lodge were the manicured greens of a golf course and to the left of the main building was a helipad. She understood from Kim that the place also sported tennis courts, swimming pool and stables.

Now this was the life.

Once again dressed in her new suede boots and Southwestern chic outfit, Irish got out of the Mercedes and strode through the huge, carved front door. The two-story room was both sumptuous and rustic, very masculine with massive beams and stone floors. A bar took up most of one side and a restaurant the other. Both were made private by a variety of screens and plants and statuary, including Irish noted, several rough-hewn animals, which looked remarkably like those at Pete's Trading Post.

Straight ahead was a desk. She headed for it.

A busty blonde, who couldn't have been more than eighteen, smiled brightly as Irish approached. "Good morning. May I help you?" A gold star pinned over the generous bosom identified her as Tami.

"Yes. I'm Irish Ellison. I had an appointment with Jackson Crow on Friday, but I was delayed and missed him. Is he in now?"

"Why, yes he surely is. You're the writer for *Esprit*, aren't you? I just love that magazine. I read almost every issue from cover to cover." She squinted at Irish. "And you sure do look familiar. I bet I've seen your picture in it somewheres. Jackson was just sick that he missed you the other day, but the gang was hoopin' and hollerin' to get gone to Dallas, and he had to leave. He's on the phone to his cousin right now, but I'll tell him you're here. Have a seat. Want some coffee?"

"No, thanks."

Irish was too nervous to sit down. Instead she grabbed a nearby chair back, took deep breaths and tried to relax. D-day was here. She was about to meet her future, and she wanted to make a good impression on Jackson Crow.

She heard a feminine giggle and a masculine chuckle behind her. Turning quickly she saw a tall, dark-haired man who had Tami's neck in a hammer-lock. He whispered in Tami's cute little ear, and she giggled again.

When the man spotted Irish, he smiled broadly and murmured something to Tami, who tried to control her giggles and hurried to her desk. The man, a class-A hunk in black boots and low-slung jeans, strolled toward Irish, his eyes assessing her as if she were a prize mare at auction, his mouth continuing to smile. He wore a starched dress shirt in pink and white stripes, the cuffs turned back and the collar open. The pastel colors merely emphasized his dark masculinity. There were no chains around his neck, but he wore a heavy gold link bracelet that must have weighed two pounds.

Wow, what a man.

"Ah, Miss Ellison, I imagine that you could cut my...heart out about now, and I deserve it for bringing even a moment's distress to such a lovely lady." He took her hand in both of his big warm ones, gazed directly into her eyes and brought her fingers briefly to his lips. "I'm Jackson Crow, the scoundrel who stood you up on Friday. I could offer a hundred good excuses, but none would compensate properly. I can only throw myself on your mercy and try my damnedest to make it up to you. You can stand me on the ninth green and take a cat-o'-nine-tails to my bare back if you want to. If you don't do it, my sister probably will."

Irish laughed at the charming rogue whose dark eyes flashed with merriment the entire time he fed her his line of malarkey. "I don't think public flogging will be necessary, Mr. Crow. The fault was mine. I was late, and you had guests to attend to. No harm done."

"Call me Jackson. And I'll call you Irish." He tucked her hand into the crook of his arm. "Welcome to Crow's Nest, Irish. I've put you in the best suite in the lodge. Let's go see if you approve. Tami, honey, rustle up Buddy and tell him to fetch Miss Ellison's bags and deliver them to three-ten."

Jackson kept up a smooth line of patter as they took the small elevator to the third floor wing. He was one of those people who had the gift of making you think that his total focus was on you. He was warm, witty and unbelievably good-looking. Almost as handsome as Kyle, but in a different way.

And the guy was very well-heeled. He had millions and millions of dollars.

Tall, dark, handsome, charming *and* rich. What more could a girl ask for?

Maybe, if what Kyle said was true, he did drink too much occasionally, but he seemed perfectly sober at the moment. She was more concerned about his behavior with Tami. He had acted very familiar with the busty little blonde. If Jackson liked them young and nubile, Irish was in trouble. She had at least ten or twelve years on Tami. And her cup size was considerably closer to the beginning of the alphabet.

When Jackson threw open the door of three-ten and they walked inside, what she saw took Irish's breath away.

From the stone fireplace to the exquisite paintings on the walls, she could only describe the suite as rustic opulence. There were no paint-by-numbers hanging here. And the view from the expansive glass windows was breathtaking. Beyond the golf course laid out amid trees and two small lakes, rolling hills forested in a dozen shades of green stretched as far as she could see.

Interspersed among the woods were small clearings where the black grasshopperlike machines bobbed up and down.

"What are those?" she asked, pointing to one near the first tee. "The black machines, I mean."

"Pumping units. For oil."

Her mouth formed an O. "Yours?"

He shrugged. "The family's." He glanced over his shoulder. "Oh, Buddy, put Miss Ellison's bags in the bedroom."

A tall, gangly young man who looked about Tami's age, nodded to them and carried Irish's bags to the other room.

"Will this place do?" Jackson asked.

"Perfectly. It's beautiful."

"Great. I'll leave you to get settled. I'm just across the hall if you need anything. Everybody will be at lunch in about an hour, and you can meet all the guys then. I'm sure that you're anxious to get on with it."

"Get on with it?"

"Gathering material for your article."

"Oh, my article. Yes, of course."

"Do you want to schedule interviews or handle things more informally?"

"I, uh, thought that I'd just sort of hang around for a while and see what happens. Be sort of a fly on the wall."

Jackson grinned. "Nobody would ever mistake you for a fly."

"Why thank you, kind sir."

"Not at all. I'll see you downstairs in an hour."

As soon as Jackson left, Irish checked the door locks and was relieved to see that besides the regular lock, there were a formidable-looking dead bolt and a flip-latch as well. When all were secure, she checked the windows, too. Silly, she knew, when she was on the third floor, but she felt better knowing they were locked.

The French doors to the balcony were a bit of a problem, but she resolved the dilemma by moving the couch up against them.

Maybe she was a little paranoid, okay, maybe she was a lot paranoid, but her therapist had assured her that her obsession was reasonably normal under the circumstances and would gradually diminish over time. She'd learned to cope as best she could and live with it. Besides, she couldn't afford a psychologist any longer.

Kyle jerked up the receiver on the first ring. "Hello."

"You must have been sitting on the telephone, cuz," Jackson said. "Anxious, are we?"

"Can it, Jackson. What about Irish?"

"She's all settled in her suite, the one right across from me on the third floor. She's some kind of beautiful woman. I could really go for her in a big way."

"Back off, buddy, or you're dead."

Jackson laughed. "I've never known you to get so riled up over a female. I can hardly believe it."

"Believe it. She's special to me. Very special. You didn't tell her that we were cousins or that Pete was your grandfather, did you?"

"The subject never came up. Now you want to explain to me what this is all about? I must have missed something before. Why don't you want to claim kin to me anymore? I haven't done anything to blacken the family name lately, have I?"

"Not in the last hour or so—that I know about." Kyle chuckled, then filled his cousin in on Irish and her intentions as well as his own plans. "Will you go along with me on this?"

"If that's what you want, but the whole mess sounds senseless to me. Seems like you could save yourself a lot of trouble if you would just tell her the truth, and the two of you could ride off into the sunset together and live happily ever after.''

"This is important to me, Jackson. Will you play it my way?''

"Sure. And I'll tell the staff to keep a lid on it as well. Matt is driving down from Dallas. He plans to visit with Grandpa Pete before he comes here. You can fill him in when he arrives.''

"He's already here, and I've filled him in, but I don't trust that brother of yours as far as I could throw his new fudge factory. Keep an eye on him, will you?''

"I'll do it. How is Grandpa healing?''

"Amazingly well. I'm taking him to see his orthopedist early this afternoon, and I've hired a nurse and a physical therapist to live in for the next week or so. The nurse has already arrived, and I've moved my stuff out to one of the tepees so that he can have my room upstairs. Alma Jane and Jenny are taking care of the trading post business.''

"Don't forget that since Smith canceled on us that we're counting on you to fill out the third foursome for the golf tournament tomorrow,'' Jackson said.

"I haven't forgotten, but I'm not as good a golfer as my brother is, and I haven't played much in the last six months.''

"Don't hand me that line. I'm not biting. You and Smith could always beat the pants off Matt and me.''

Remembering all the times that the two pairs of

brothers had gone head-to-head in competition, Kyle chuckled. "That's true. I'll see you at Crow's Nest this evening."

Irish had unpacked her bags, and she'd spent another five or ten minutes admiring the view before she became restless. She hadn't come here to admire the scenery; she'd come hunting, and she had research to do before lunch. After checking her makeup, she grabbed her notebook and went downstairs to pump Tami for information.

Pumping Tami turned out to be more difficult than Irish anticipated. While the little blonde may have given the impression that she was a bubblehead, Irish soon learned that behind all Tami's cutesy drawling and eyelash fluttering was a sharp mind and a tenacious determination to guard the privacy of the lodge's guests.

Irish learned only a little more about the gathering of wealthy men. The lodge's only guests were a dozen members of a special group of Texas millionaires under the age of forty. All of them were single, but according to Tami, several of them were in serious relationships or engaged.

"I'm afraid that I can't tell you any more about our guests," Tami said, "except that they're all very nice men." She giggled. "Course they do get a little rambunctious at times, but that's just because they like to come here and let their hair down among friends. Anything personal about them would have to come from

Jackson or the gentlemen themselves, you understand.'' She leaned close and whispered, ''I know I could trust you, but if I said one word, I'd be fired in a minute—even if Jackson was the best man at my mama and daddy's wedding. And I love this job. Nothing around here pays as good, and Jimmy and Paulie and I need the money.''

''Jimmy and Paulie?''

''Jimmy's my husband and Paulie's my little boy. This is a picture of them.'' She handed Irish a framed snapshot. ''Jimmy's going to school at the Junior College and works here at the stable in the afternoon, and my mother keeps Paulie during the day. Paulie was six months old when this picture was taken. He's almost nine months old now, and he'll be walking before you know it.''

Irish left the desk knowing the intimate details of Paulie's teething process and motor abilities, and even how Tami's mother made the county's best blackberry jelly, but almost nothing about the young millionaires.

No matter, she told herself as she went outside to stroll around the grounds. She was really only interested in Jackson.

As she walked, images of Kyle kept intruding on her thoughts. She pushed them away. Not Kyle. Jackson. Jackson Crow was the man for her.

He was a handsome devil.

And rich as sin.

Perfect. He was perfect. Exactly what she was looking for.

Except for one tiny little thing, and that was hardly worth mentioning.

So he didn't turn her on like a house afire immediately. Instant attraction was vastly overrated. Irish was sure that, with time, that part of their relationship would grow and develop. After all, Jackson was a very charming and virile man. She was sure that their first kiss would rev up her libido.

And if for some remote reason that it didn't, well, there would be almost a dozen other eligible millionaires to choose from. In fact, she planned to study the entire group very carefully. She wasn't eliminating any possibilities at this point.

The path she followed led her to a short footbridge arched over a lazy stream. She stopped, leaned against the rail and watched the trickle of clear water run along an irregular, sandy path strewn with small rocks striated in shades of rust and gray.

How peaceful it was here. How secure she felt among the tall pines whispering overhead. Being in this place was like being in another world.

Irish closed her eyes, listened to the soft sounds of birds and breathed in deeply, savoring the clean, crisp scents of the wooded area and thinking how very far away from her old life that she was here.

"Well, hello there, gorgeous," a masculine voice said. "Where have you been all my life?"

Startled, Irish whirled around.

Seven

At first Irish thought that it was Jackson who had spoken to her, but on second glance she saw that this man was younger than Jackson. He was tall with similar dark hair and eyes, but the planes of his face were softer, and he had a deep cleft in his chin. He, too, had on boots and jeans, but he wore a rugby shirt.

"Oh, hello," she said. "You startled me. I didn't realize that anyone was around."

"I just dumped my bags in the cabin over there. I can only hope that we're neighbors."

"Neighbors?"

"Are you staying in one of the cabins?"

"No," she said. "I'm in the main lodge."

"Well, shoot! I was hoping I could borrow a cup

of sugar or something tonight." He gave her a totally disarming grin and held out a small gold sack. "I'm Matt Crow. Share my fudge?"

"I'm Irish Ellison, and thanks, I adore fudge." She took a small piece from the bag and popped it into her mouth. "Mmmmm. Scrumptious."

He offered the bag again. "Best fudge in the world, don't you think?"

"I've never tasted better, but I don't dare have another piece. I might wrestle you for the entire bag."

Matt laughed. "I like you, Irish Ellison. You're a woman after my own heart. You must be the writer."

"I am. And you must be Jackson's brother."

"Guilty as charged. I was just about to go up to the lodge for lunch. Join me?" When she hesitated, he folded the candy sack shut and handed it to her. "Consider it a bribe."

"I wouldn't want to take it all."

"I have a lot more in my cabin." His boyish grin was totally disarming. "And if that's not enough, I own the whole fudge factory."

He offered his arm, and she took it. "A whole fudge factory?"

"Yes, ma'am."

"How absolutely decadent." As they walked she learned that Matt, who started out to be an attorney, also had vast timber interests as well as Crow Airlines, a wild and crazy, no-frills airline based in Dallas.

"The Crow with all the black airplanes?" Irish asked.

"Black with told trim. Yep, that's me. 'As the Crow flies' is our motto. Ever flown with us?"

"No, I don't think so."

"You would remember if you had. The pilots wear cowboy hats and jeans, and the attendants wear denim overalls. We serve drinks and sunflower seeds. If you want a meal, you have to bring it with you, and if you want reserved seating, go Continental, but you can't beat our prices or our reputation for being on time. And we've never had a major accident."

"Never?" she asked as they climbed the steps to the lodge.

"Nope. Cheap doesn't mean unsafe. We have the finest crews and the best equipment in the world."

"You're proud of the airline, aren't you?"

"Yes, ma'am, I am right proud." He held open the door.

Two men were standing just inside the lodge. One was tall and thin; the other was two inches shorter than Irish and wore thick glasses. The short one said, "Leave it to you, Matt, to find a good-lookin' woman at a bachelor party."

Matt grinned. "Some of us have it, Harve, and some of us only dream. Irish, this is Harve Dudley and Bob Willis. Irish is here to write about us for—what's the name of that magazine, Irish?"

"*Esprit.*" She shook hands with the two men. Bob, a shy, quiet man, was into land and cattle; Harve had several large automobile dealerships.

"You need a new Cadillac, darlin'? I'm your man."

"Down, boy," Matt said. "Esther Ann will trim your wick in a New York minute." Harve only laughed as Matt explained to Irish that Esther Ann was his fiancée of eight years. "She says that the only reason that Harve won't marry her is because he'll have to drop out of our club."

Before, during, and immediately after lunch, Irish met another half-dozen or more of the millionaires: two Jims—one who was called Jim and one who went by Mac—Carlton, Aaron, Noah, Mitch, and Vernon, who was better known as Spud. Their business involvements covered the spectrum from rice farming to banking to bridge building. One of the men, either Mac or Noah—she'd have to check that later—was into ocean salvage, which sounded fascinating. An interesting, energetic group. This was absolute heaven for someone looking for an eligible millionaire.

In between meeting and being charming to so many matrimonial prospects, Irish made notes furiously, trying to keep all the men straight. Too, she was going to have to write an article for the magazine to keep her honest.

"One of our members is missing," Matt told her. "My cousin Smith grows cows and grapefruit down in the Rio Grande Valley, but he couldn't make it this time. Something going on with his computer company. We had to talk—"

"Dammit, Matt!" Jackson said, scowling at his brother.

"What did I say?" Matt looked mystified.

"Quit hogging all of this beautiful lady's attention. Why don't you go find Harve? He's getting together a poker game." Jackson took Irish's hand and looped it through the crook of his arm and gave her a mega-kilowatt smile. "Let me show you the swimming pool and the stables. Do you ride?"

Irish should have lied. She should have told Jackson that she didn't know one end of a horse from the other. She wouldn't be in such agony now. Instead she'd told him that she rode a little and was anxious to learn to ride with a Western saddle.

He'd spent several hours trying to teach her.

Riding horses was unnatural.

The insides of her legs were raw. Her butt throbbed. No doubt her tailbone was fractured from the jarring experience, and she was sure that her hip was dislocated. She ground her teeth to keep from hobbling and tried her best to continue smiling all the way back to the lodge.

"Are you sure that you're okay?" Jackson asked.

"Absolutely. I'm fine."

"Then how about a drink at the bar?"

"Maybe later," she said brightly. All she could think of was hot water and the Jacuzzi. With her eye trained on the elevator, she squared her shoulders and went straight to it before her wobbly knees buckled.

Once inside, she punched three and grabbed the support rail. She closed her eyes and tried to endure the distressed messages from her nerve endings.

"Well, fancy meeting you here," a sexy male voice said.

Her eyes popped open. "Kyle!"

He grinned. "In the flesh."

"What are *you* doing here?"

"Riding up on the elevator with you."

"I can see that. I meant why are you at Crow's Nest?"

"I was invited."

"Invited? By whom?"

The door whisked open before he answered. "By Jackson Crow. I've known him all my life. We grew up together."

"But only members of the millionaires club are here."

Kyle held open the elevator door and motioned for Irish to precede him. She dropped all pretense and hobbled to her suite while she could still walk.

"I know, but one of the members is absent, and they need someone to take his place in the golf tournament. Jackson knows that I'm a pretty fair golfer, so he invited me. Plus, I thought that you might need some help."

"Help? Me?"

"Sure. If you're determined to snag a millionaire husband, I thought that I might be able to give you a few pointers, sort of act as a consultant. Why are you limping, honey? Did you have an accident? Those high-heeled boots are right pretty, but not very practical around here on this rough ground."

Irish gritted her teeth as she fumbled her key in the lock. "No, I didn't have an accident. I've been horse-back riding, and I'm a little stiff. I'll be fine as soon as I have a long soak and about three fingers of gin. And I don't need a consultant, thank you very much."

"Looks like you could use a masseur."

"Desperately," she admitted, wincing. "Is there one available?"

"I'll see if I can rustle up one. You go soak."

"Thanks, Kyle, you're a sweetheart."

"Glad to oblige. What are friends for?"

Irish felt her thighs and calves begin to quiver, and she stripped off her jacket and hurried to the bathroom before all her muscles decided to cramp into a scream-ing mass of knotted misery.

She turned on the water in the tub full force, sat down on a vanity bench to pull off her boots and yelped. Loudly. She tried another tactic. Sweat popped out on her upper lip, and she groaned.

Kyle rapped on the door. "Irish, are you okay?"

"No."

"Anything I can do to help?"

She wanted to tell him, "No, absolutely not," and to go away. That way she could salvage her pride. But the truth was that she needed him desperately. She couldn't soak in the tub wearing boots and jeans, and she couldn't get those damned boots off alone.

"Irish?"

"*What?*" she said crossly.

"Honey, do you need any help?"

"I'm not your honey, and yes, I need help."

After a pause, he asked, "May I come in?"

She sighed. "I suppose that you'll have to." When he opened the door, she glared at him. "Don't you dare laugh."

"I'm not laughing. What's wrong?"

"Four hours on a medieval torture device wouldn't have been any more wretched than sitting on the back of that blasted horse."

"*Four hours!* And you've never ridden before?"

She shook her head.

"What fool took a greenhorn riding for four hours?"

"Jackson. But it's not his fault. I told him that I could ride. Although I'm sure that he probably figured out that I was stretching the truth a tiny bit when I fell off the horse the second time."

"The *second* time?"

"Well, the first time I was totally humiliated, but Jackson said it could have happened to anybody. The horse stepped in a hole and stumbled. I'm not sure what happened the last time, but Jackson said that maybe we'd better call it a day. I can't tell you how relieved I was. I can't believe that people actually enjoy riding those beasts."

Kyle cursed softly and turned off the water. "How can I help?"

"I—I can't bend to get my boots off. Please don't laugh at me."

"I wouldn't laugh for the world." He knelt at her feet and carefully removed her boots.

She wiggled her toes. "Ah, heaven."

"Can you manage your jeans?"

"I think so."

"Let's see if you can."

Irish, who was used to dressing and undressing in front of throngs of people for doing runway work, suddenly turned shy. "Turn your back."

Kyle rolled his eyes, but he complied.

She unfastened the tight jeans and got them halfway down before she ran into trouble. At the first grunt of discomfort, Kyle cursed again and turned around to help.

"Kyle!"

"Forget modesty. If you don't work on those kinks now, by tomorrow morning you won't be able to get out of bed. Think of me as a doctor."

She had no choice. Poker stiff, she allowed him to take off her jeans. Without a word, she grabbed a towel, wrapped it around her middle and pulled down her panties from beneath it. She stared straight ahead as he removed those as well.

"Thank you," she said primly. "I can handle the rest."

"Are you sure?"

"Positive. Thank you."

"Can you get in the tub by yourself?"

"Yes, I'll manage. Thank you." She expected Kyle to leave, but he didn't. Instead he started rummaging around in the bathroom cabinets. "What are you looking for?"

"Epsom salts, but I can't find any. Jackson will probably have some in his suite. I'll check."

"Kyle Rutledge, don't you *dare* tell him what you want it for. He'll think that I'm an absolute ninny."

He dropped a kiss on her nose. "Don't worry, darlin'. My lips are sealed."

"I'm not your *darlin'!* We're merely friends and don't you forget it."

"Yes, ma'am." He had the audacity to grin.

She waited until he left to finish undressing and get into the tub. With laborious effort plus a few grunts and groans, she finally made it. As soon as she lowered herself into the hot water, she felt better. When the jets began to agitate the water and massage her aching parts, it was sheer ecstasy. She dumped a bit of fragrant oil in the churning bath, leaned back, and savored the feeling.

"Ahhhhh."

For several minutes, she couldn't even think. She relaxed and drifted in a sea of soothing sensation.

"Feeling better?"

Irish squealed and crossed her arms in front of her. "Kyle! What are you doing in here?"

He held up a large box the size of a half-gallon milk container. "Epsom salts. Guaranteed to reduce soreness. Jackson had lots of it. And I didn't breathe a word to him about you."

"Thank you. Now would you please leave and allow me some privacy?"

"In a minute. I have to dump this stuff in the water with you. As I said before, just think of me as a doctor."

Wearing a light blue Western shirt that emphasized the color of his gorgeous eyes, low-slung jeans that emphasized his manhood and a lopsided smile that emphasized his sexiness, he didn't look a thing like any doctor she'd ever met. "I—I find that difficult."

He winked. "Then just think of me as a good friend. We're friends, aren't we?"

"Yes."

"There ya go." He opened the box and slowly poured the white crystals around her. When there was a knock at the door of her suite, he said, "You relax and I'll get that."

"But Kyle, I don't want anyone to find you—"

"Don't worry about it. It's just the bartender with the drinks."

"What drinks?" she asked. But he was gone.

In a couple of minutes he returned with a tray. "You mentioned gin. Are gimlets okay?"

"Gimlets are terrific."

He filled two glass from the pitcher and set them on the rim of the tub. "Drink those and relax for about a half hour, and I'll arrange things for your massage."

She took a sip of the first drink. It was ice-cold, tart, and perfect. "Ahhh, wonderful. So you were able to arrange a masseuse on such short notice?"

"Everything's taken care of, hon—Irish. Just relax and leave it to me."

Irish tucked the bath sheet around her and poked her head out the bathroom door. Kyle sat in an easy chair, reading a magazine. She didn't see anyone else.

Kyle glanced up, smiled and laid the magazine aside as he stood. "Ready for the massage?"

She stepped into the room and looked around. "Where's the masseuse?"

"Masseur. And you're looking at him. The oil is warmed and everything is ready." He motioned toward the bed where the covers were turned back suggestively and an extra sheet was doubled and spread over one side. A stack of towels and an assortment of bottles were on the night table.

"Oh, no. No way," she said, backing away as he approached.

"But, honey, I give a great massage. Honest."

Her mouth went dry at the notion, and her heart started pumping like crazy. "I don't think that your giving me a massage is…is appropriate."

"Why not? We're friends."

"Friends, yes, but this is too intimate. I don't think it would be smart. I told you that I'm here to find a rich husband, and that's what I mean to do."

"I don't see the problem."

"Then you're an idiot. You know very well that we—"

One side of his mouth twitched. "That we—what? Strike more sparks than a welding torch?"

She gathered her bath sheet closer. "Certainly not! I've told you a dozen times that we can't be any more than friends. You need to get that through your head."

"You don't have to yell, darlin'. I get the message. We're only friends and can never be any more than that because I'm not rich enough for you, and you don't want me rubbing you down because you're afraid that having my hands all over your body will turn you on and confuse things. Right?"

"Yes! No! In your dreams, buster! Give me the damned massage." She stuck her nose in the air. "I'll just think of you as a doctor." She strode to the bed and plopped down on her stomach. "And don't call me darlin'."

"Okay, sweetheart."

He whisked away the bath sheet, and she stifled a yelp. Before she could protest, he draped a warm, dry towel over her buttocks. "I'll start with your feet," he said, lifting her left foot and spreading warm lotion over it.

Feet were okay. She could handle him massaging her feet.

A moment later, she changed her mind. She never realized that feet could be an erogenous zone.

When he moved up to ankles and calves, she ground her teeth to keep from sighing with pleasure. With every stroke of his wonderful, magical hands, images flooded her brain.

PLAY THE

LUCKY

SLOT MACHINE GAME!

...AND YOU CAN GET FREE Books!
PLUS A FREE Gift!

PLAY "LUCKY 7" AND GET
FIVE FREE GIFTS!

HOW TO PLAY:

1. With a coin, carefully scratch off the silver box at the right. Then check the claim chart to see what we have for you—**FREE BOOKS** and a gift—**ALL YOURS! ALL FREE!**

2. Send back this card and you'll receive brand-new Silhouette Desire® novels. These books have a cover price of $3.50 each, but they are yours to keep absolutely free.

3. There's no catch. You're under no obligation to buy anything. We charge nothing— ZERO—for your first shipment And you don't have to make any minimum number of purchases—not even one!

4. The fact is thousands of readers enjoy receiving books by mail from the Silhouette Reader Service™ months before they're available in stores. They like the convenience of home delivery and they love our discount prices!

5. We hope that after receiving your free books you'll want to remain a subscriber. But the choice is yours—to continue or cancel, any time at all! So why not take us up on our invitation, with no risk of any kind. You'll be glad you did!

YOURS FREE!

This beautiful porcelain box is topped with a lovely bouquet of porcelain flowers, perfect for holding rings, pins or other precious trinkets— and is yours ABSOLUTELY FREE when you accept our NO-RISK offer!

NOT ACTUAL SIZE

PLAY THE

LUCKY 7

SLOT MACHINE GAME!

Just scratch off the silver box with a coin. Then check below to see the gifts you get!

YES!

I have scratched off the silver box. Please send me all the gifts for which I qualify. I understand I am under no obligation to purchase any books, as explained on the back and on the opposite page.

225 CIS A7YH
(U-SIL-D-05/97)

Name

Address   Apt.#

City   State   Zip

7	7	7	**WORTH FOUR FREE BOOKS PLUS A FREE TRINKET BOX!**
🍒	🍒	🍒	**WORTH THREE FREE BOOKS!**
♣	♣	♣	**WORTH TWO FREE BOOKS!**
🔔	🔔	🍒	**WORTH ONE FREE BOOK!**

DETACH AND MAIL CARD TODAY!

The Silhouette Reader Service™ —Here's how it works

Accepting free books places you under no obligation to buy anything. You may keep the books and gift and return the shipping statement marked "cancel." If you do not cancel, about a month later we'll send you 6 additional novels, and bill you just $2.90 each, plus 25¢ delivery per book and applicable sales tax, if any.* That's the complete price—and compared to cover prices of $3.50 each—quite a bargain! You may cancel at any time, but if you choose to continue, every month we'll send you 6 more books, which you may either purchase at the discount price...or return to us and cancel your subscription.

*Terms and prices subject to change without notice. Sales tax applicable in N.Y.

Wild images.

Erotic images.

His long fingers stroked soothing balm higher up her legs, and she almost came off the bed. Dear Lord, could she endure this?

When his hands gently kneaded the inside of her thighs, her whole body began to quiver, and she felt herself go wet.

"Just relax," he murmured.

"I am relaxed!"

He only chuckled.

Damn him and his sexy chuckle. And his sensuous fingers. Despite her best intentions, under his ministrations she did finally start to relax. Tension began loosening its hold on her body.

But when he suddenly straddled her lower legs, she stiffened. "What are you *doing?*"

"*Shhhh*. Just shifting to get better access."

Likely story. She ought to kick him out of her room. Now. This instant. But the warm, tingly lotion and his glorious touch across her back and down her spine felt too fantastic for her to object.

The knots let go.

Her muscles became supple, and his strokes became slow and sinuous. She felt as if she were floating on a sea of marshmallow cream as his hands performed their hypnotic sorcery.

And when he removed the towel that draped her and stroked lower, more intimately, she was too mellowed out to protest.

Eight

Long after Kyle felt Irish's muscles go slack, he continued to massage her gently, relishing the feel of her silky softness beneath his fingers. Her skin, the color of fine porcelain touched with honey, was unblemished except for faint blue splotches from the fall on her hip and three small moles that formed a triangle on her right shoulder blade.

Intriguing little moles that begged his touch.

He brushed the spot lightly with the pads of his fingers. The simple exploration didn't satisfy him. He wanted to press his lips against her warm skin and taste her with his tongue, but he didn't dare. She trusted him.

"Irish," he whispered.

She didn't stir. Bless her heart, she was sound asleep. His hands stilled, and he studied the side of her face that was turned toward him. With her makeup washed away, the scars on her left cheek were faintly visible. Knowing what pain that she must have endured, both physically and emotionally, angered him. What demented degenerate could have wantonly inflicted such agony?

Tremendous feelings of tenderness welled up from his chest and caught in his throat. He couldn't abide the idea of anyone hurting Irish again, of anyone crushing her vibrant spirit or causing her one moment's suffering. Even Jackson's stunt with the horseback riding made him furious. A potent sense of protectiveness unfurled inside him, a sense so strong that it was almost palpable, and brought a strange urge to take up a shield and sword and stand in front of her to slay dragons and be her champion.

When he thought of her reaction if he told her his feelings, he smiled. She would have a fit. Still, the feelings were there. Odd feelings that he'd never experienced before.

Maybe, for the first time in his life, Kyle Rutledge was truly falling in love. He couldn't explain why it had happened now, with this woman, but he couldn't deny the intense emotions she stirred in him.

Very carefully, he leaned over and touched his lips to the little triangle of moles, then eased off the bed and pulled the sheet over her. She needed to rest. He'd check on her later.

After he adjusted the blinds to darken the room, he picked up his boots and slipped quietly out of the suite.

Just as he eased the latch to, a hand clamped on his shoulder. "Caught ya with your boots in your hand," Jackson said, chuckling. "Been stealing a little nooky from the lovely lady?"

Sudden anger blazed up in Kyle like the flash of a back draft in a burning building. "You bastard!" Before he thought, he drew back and punched his cousin.

Jackson staggered and caught himself against a wall. Rubbing his chin, he frowned at Kyle. "What the hell was that for?"

"You've got a nasty mouth and a nasty mind, and you almost killed Irish on that damned horse. She can barely walk."

"Hey, man, I'm sorry for what I said. I was just kidding you. It was a joke."

Kyle scowled. "You don't see me laughing. And what the hell did you mean taking a greenhorn riding for four hours? You must have realized right away that she couldn't ride."

"Yeah, I did, but dammit, Kyle, every man on the place was salivating over her. Including Matt. I was trying to protect your interests and keep her away from the pack. Some of these guys are fast movers. Taking her riding seemed like a good idea at the time, and she said that she knew how. By the time I saw that she didn't know one end of a horse from the other, I didn't want to embarrass her by calling her a liar. Is she really hurt?''

''Hell, yes, she's hurt. She's bruised and can barely walk.''

''Maybe I'd better call a doctor.''

''Jackson, I *am* a doctor.''

''Oh, yeah. But you're a plastic surgeon.''

''It doesn't take an orthopedic specialist to recognize a bruised butt. I swear to God, for a smart man, sometimes you can be dumber than a box of rocks. I hope she sues you for stupidity.''

Jackson grinned. ''You're really crazy about her, aren't you?''

Kyle sucked in a big breath, then blew it out slowly, rested his hands on his hips and dropped his head. ''Yes. Yes, I am. But she's dead set on marrying a millionaire, and these next few days with her loose among so many hot prospects may do me in.''

''Talk about *dumb*,'' Jackson said. ''I don't see why you don't just tell the woman that you're loaded and ease your misery.''

''I explained that to you already. I have my reasons for not wanting her to know yet, so you keep your mouth shut, cuz. And, by the way, she doesn't want you to know that she's hurt, either, so don't let on and humiliate her.''

''Right. Any other instructions, doctor?''

Kyle chuckled. ''That about covers it. Thanks, Jackson. Sorry about your jaw. Want me to make you an ice pack?''

"Naw, I'll live."

"Where do I bunk?"

"Your suite's right there, next door to Irish." Jackson motioned with his thumb over his shoulder. "Buddy already stowed your gear. Come on downstairs with me. There's a hot poker game going, and I feel lucky."

Irish wasn't sure what woke her. It might have been hunger or the scent of roses or the flush of an erotic dream, but something stirred her from sleep. She glanced at the clock and was dismayed to discover that it was almost eight. No wonder that her stomach was acting up. If she didn't hurry, she would miss dinner altogether.

When she pulled back the covers, she found that she was nude. As soon as she remembered how she'd gotten that way, she groaned. Had she really let Kyle give her a massage? Laid there without a stitch on except for a tiny towel?

What lunacy! No wonder she'd had an erotic dream. His touch had been pure sorcery. She hadn't liked the way his hands on her had made her feel—or rather she had liked it too much. And it had to stop.

Dreading to move, she glanced at the clock again. That's when she noticed the flowers and note on the bedside table. Bright yellow wildflowers, a little droopy, filled a water glass. A note was propped beside it.

From Kyle. Saying that he would see her at dinner.

How sweet.

Despite her best efforts a tender smile formed when she thought of him picking flowers for her.

No! Forget about Kyle. Think of Jackson. Or Jim or Aaron or even Spud. They're the ones with the bank accounts. Think mansion in Dallas or Houston or San Antonio. Think Cadillac or BMW. Think diamonds. Don't think of Kyle picking wildflowers.

Moving slowly, she sat up. She was stiff and sore, but only moderately so. She eased off the bed and stood. So far, so good. When she went to the bathroom for her robe, she was pleasantly surprised to discover that she could walk without hobbling.

Kyle had worked wonders with her aching and bruised parts. But that was the last time she would allow him to touch her so intimately. He was a distraction, a major deviation from her plan.

She carefully applied her makeup, then quickly donned sexy silk pants and a top in a vibrant green that was one of her most flattering colors. As soon as she finished dressing, she hurried from her bedroom, then stopped dead still.

The sitting room was filled with flowers. Red roses mostly. There were six bouquets of roses, four red and two yellow. None of the arrangements held less than two dozen long-stemmed buds. When she read all the cards, she found that one yellow bouquet was from Jackson welcoming her to Texas and to Crow's Nest. The other yellow arrangement was from Mitch Harris, who, if she remembered correctly, was the ex-pro football player who raised horses. The note asked her to join him for dinner.

The red roses were from Jim, Aaron, Carlton and Spud, all accompanied by requests for dinner.

On the coffee table was a huge, gold foil-wrapped box from Matt Crow along with a note telling her that there was lots more where this came from. She laughed, not needing to undo the wrapping to know that he'd sent about ten pounds of fudge.

Another small box, wrapped in the same foil paper, sat beside a bottle of champagne—Dom Pérignon, no less. Inside the box was a hammered gold figure the shape of Texas, suspended on a delicate gold chain. A diamond—or a very convincing fake—was set in at a spot about where Dallas would be. This was from Noah Birchfield, who welcomed her to Texas and said that he would love to show her Dallas, but in the meantime, would she share the effervescence of her presence and the champagne with him later?

Oh, ho. Very smooth.

Noah Birchfield. Dallas. Banking? Yes, banking and insurance.

Going a little bald.

But, hey, hair wasn't everything. She'd always heard that bald men were demons in the bedroom. Noah was definitely on the A list.

As she fastened the chain around her neck, Irish mentally ticked off the list of eligible bachelors. Every one of them had sent flowers or a gift except Harve, Bob and Mac. Not bad. Not bad at all. Jackson was still her first choice, but in case that didn't pan out, there were seven other Texas millionaires interested.

Very heady stuff. Great for a gal's ego. Delight tripped a little bubble of laugher and a big smile.

As she turned to leave, there was a soft knock on her door. Before she could cross the room, she heard a key in the lock, and her heart caught as the door slowly opened.

Dear God, she hadn't bolted the door!

Panic paralyzed her. The door swung open.

She yelped; the intruder yelped.

The intruder, a slightly past middle-aged blonde who needed a root touch-up, splayed her hand across her chest. "Oh, my gosh, I'm sorry. I thought you were still asleep. You nearly scared me out of ten years growth. I'm Pat. I work here, and I've about run my legs off delivering all these flowers and things and trying not to disturb you. That Kyle said he'd skin me within an inch of my life if I did, and I believed him." She laughed, a hearty, brassy laugh from her belly that, along with the twinkle in her eyes, was warm and completely unaffected.

Liking Pat immediately, Irish smiled. "Oh, I doubt if he would actually skin you."

"I doubt it, too, but I really didn't want to wake you. He said you weren't feeling well, but all those boys downstairs were chomping at the bit to send you the roses and other geegaws. Good thing I found some wrapping paper left over from last Christmas." She glanced down at the foil-wrapped package in her hand.

"I ran out of the plain gold, and I hope you'll overlook the holly sprigs, but Mac insisted you have this right away. I guess he didn't want the others to beat him out. They're a competitive bunch. Here ya go." Pat handed her the package.

"Thanks. It was very sweet of you to go to so much trouble."

"No trouble, honey. I was glad to do it. You coming down to dinner pretty soon? Not a one of them will eat until you get there, and they need some meat and potatoes to sop up all that Jack Daniel's they been drinkin'."

Irish laughed. "I'll be down in a couple of minutes."

Pat left, and Irish opened the package. Inside was a book by Mac about finding a treasure galleon. He had written a flowery inscription, declaring her more lovely than any chest of pirate's booty. A shiny gold doubloon was tucked between the pages.

She smiled, flipped the coin in the air and caught it. Make that eight other interested millionaires. Tucking the doubloon in her bra for luck, she left the suite humming "Diamonds Are a Girl's Best Friend."

Kyle knew the minute that she entered the room. He knew, not because of any sort of extrasensory awareness, but because Spud Hall stopped dead in the middle of the punch line of the raunchy joke he was telling and jumped to his feet. Noah, Aaron, Mac and Carlton glanced at the doorway and scrambled up, too.

The others looked over their shoulders and hurriedly stood as well.

After about two heartbeats, every man in the bar, except Jackson and him, rushed to Irish's side, jostling and elbowing for position. Kyle had never seen anything like it. These were grown men, successful captains of industry, not teenagers fighting over tickets to a rock concert.

He shook his head and glanced at Jackson, who sat there grinning. "What's with these guys? You'd think they'd never seen a good-looking woman before."

"Well, you have to admit that Irish is a few pegs above good-looking," Jackson said. "Besides, these ol' boys are a mighty competitive bunch. I'll have to admit that I'm tempted to jump in the contest myself."

"Contest? What contest?"

"They've got a bet on to see who gets to take her to dinner. The pot's ten thousand."

Kyle scowled. "They'll probably suffocate her before she decides. Come on, help me get her out of that huddle of jerks. They're your buddies."

Jackson got to his feet and strolled to the cluster of men hustling Irish. "Okay, fellows, let's break it up and let the little lady get her breath."

"Move it, dammit," Kyle growled as he elbowed his way past Carlton Gramercy. "Give her some room."

Irish had never been so glad to see anybody as she was to see Kyle and Jackson shoving through the herd of men. She was flattered beyond belief at all the attention from such a choice group of men, in fact, she felt a bit like Scarlett O'Hara at a garden party, but she was beginning to get panicky in the presence of so much blatant testosterone.

"Thanks," she said to her rescuers. "I am a little overwhelmed by all the attention."

The men grumbled, but moved back in deference to their host. "Hell, Jackson," Spud said, "we should have figured that you'd find some way to beat our time, and you ain't even in the pot."

Kyle smiled at Irish, who felt decidedly shaky, and squeezed her hand. "All these gentlemen want to have the honor of escorting you to dinner. Why don't you put them out of their misery and pick one."

Irish looked from one expectant face to the other. Her first instinct was to select Jackson, but most of the others had been so sweet with flowers and gifts that she hated to turn them down. "How can I make such a decision?"

"Tell you what," Jackson said, snagging a black Stetson from a nearby hat rack, "why don't y'all put your names in the hat and Irish can draw. She can have dinner with one of you, coffee and dessert with another and after-dinner drinks with somebody else."

"But who wins the pot?" Mac asked.

"First pull," Jackson said. "And I'll even kick in for Kyle and me."

"What pot?" Irish whispered to Kyle.

"Small wager as to who gets to take you to dinner first."

There was more grumbling, but the men fished business cards from their pockets and tossed them in the hat Jackson held. Kyle automatically reached for his wallet to extract one of his own, then stopped. He couldn't use his card without identifying himself as Kyle Rutledge, M.D. Instead he took one of Jackson's, scratched through the printing and wrote his name on the back.

"Why are you putting your name in the hat?" Irish asked Kyle.

Kyle winked. "I could use the cash."

"Gee thanks," she said sarcastically. "I feel like the prize in a box of Cracker Jacks."

"No need for you to feel that way, ma'am," Spud said. "The bettin' is just our way of foolin' around. Just a friendly bet. Chump change. Win, lose, or draw tonight, I'd be mighty pleased if you'd have dinner with me tomorrow evening."

"Like hell she will," Aaron said. "I was planning on asking her myself."

"So was I," Mitch Harris piped up.

"Boys, boys, we can work this out later," Jackson said. "First things first." He shook the cards in the hat and offered the Stetson to Irish. "We might even talk the lovely lady into a kiss for the winner as a bonus." He winked at her and grinned.

Kyle scowled at his cousin and mumbled, "Like hell."

Irritated by Kyle's attitude, Irish smiled brightly and said, "I'd be delighted."

Grins spread through the group. Carlton Gramercy rubbed his hands together and said, "Get ready to pucker, sugar, I feel lucky."

There were several good-natured jibes at Carlton and a few comments about their own chances, but everyone grew quiet as Irish put her hand in and stirred the cards a final time.

Feeling somehow that the name of the millionaire she drew might be critical to her future, she closed her eyes, said a little prayer and took a deep breath.

Reaching into the hat that Jackson held slightly above her head, she selected one.

No, two were stuck together.

Rubbing them apart, she let one fall back into the felt crown. Her fingers shook as she pulled the winner from the hat and, too nervous to even peek, held it against her chest under her palm.

Let it be Jackson, she said over and over in a silent mantra.

"Come on, darlin'," Spud said, "don't keep us in suspense. Tell us who the lucky man is."

Irish thrust the card at Jackson. "You read it."

Jackson glanced at the name. His eyebrows lifted slightly, and a slow grin spread over his face. "Well, well, well."

Nine

Irish's eyes widened in shock. "*Kyle Rutledge?* But—but—" she sputtered.

Kyle chuckled. "Can't fight fate, darlin'."

"But—but—"

"You lucky dog," Carlton said, slapping Kyle's back. "Say, Jackson, don't put that hat up yet. We've still got to draw two more names."

"You got it. Irish, select your partner for dessert and coffee."

Irish reached again into the black Stetson and pulled out another business card. This time she looked at the name. "Vernon Hall."

"Hot damn!" Spud yelled. "That's me."

Jackson offered the hat again. "And for after-dinner drinks."

She drew another card. "Noah Birchfield."

He smiled and bowed slightly. "Then my gift was appropriate."

"It would seem so," Irish said, "but I need to put it on ice."

"I'll have Pat take care of it," Noah told her.

"Don't know what you two have going on, but it sounds downright sinful," Harve said, grinning. "Hey, Jackson, what about the rest of us? When do we get our turn?"

"Watch it," Mac said, "or I'm gonna have to call Esther Ann and tell her you're not behaving yourself."

"Not on your life. This little lady is just doing interviews for her magazine. Right, Miz Ellison?"

Irish laughed. "Right, Mr. Dudley."

"Tell you what," Jackson said, "we'll make up a schedule, draw for the slots and post it on the bulletin board tomorrow morning after breakfast."

"But who gets to take her to breakfast?" Aaron asked.

"I do," Jackson said.

"Hell, man, you didn't even draw."

Jackson laughed. "So sue me."

Kyle offered his arm to Irish. "Shall we have our dinner?"

She rolled her eyes, sighed and took his arm. "I could strangle you," she muttered as they walked to a table in a secluded alcove. "Why the devil did you put your name in the hat?"

"Told you I could use the money." He gave her

that charming, lopsided grin that always made her heart catch. "Besides, I enjoy your company."

"But you know that I'm looking for a millionaire. I've made that perfectly clear."

"You surely have, and I'm not likely to forget it. Tell you what, I'll be your consultant and give you the lowdown on all the guys here. You want to steer clear of some of them."

"I do?"

"Oh, yeah. For instance, I'll bet that Mac won't tell you that he's been in jail."

"In jail?"

"Yep." Kyle held out her chair. "If you are interested in snagging one of these guys, you're going to need my help."

When they were seated, Irish leaned forward and whispered, "Are you sure that Jackson drinks too much? I haven't noticed that he does."

"Trust me, the man's a sot. Would you prefer the fish or the steak?"

"The fish. And by the way, how much money did you win?"

"Twelve thousand."

Irish almost went into apoplexy. "Twelve thousand *dollars?"*

"Yep. You want a baked potato or the rice pilaf?"

"Rice. Do you mean that everybody put up a thousand dollars?"

"Yep. Salad?"

"With low-cal Italian dressing. Where did you get a thousand dollars?"

"I didn't. Jackson threw in for me."

"Is that fair?"

"Hell, yes, it's fair. I won, didn't I? Anyway, he said that if I'd come and play golf, he'd pay all my expenses. This was an expense. Wine?"

"Please. It still doesn't seem quite right somehow. If it was Jackson's money, then he should have the pot."

"No way. You drew my name. I won. Those were the rules. Don't worry about it, Irish. This is no big deal. Jackson's loaded."

Their conversation paused while Kyle ordered their dinner from the waiter and a large loaf of warm bread was served. The yeasty smell wafting up from the loaf was heavenly. Her stomach rumbled.

Irish cut off a big hunk and slathered it with butter. She ate half a slice to quiet her hunger pangs, then leaned forward again and said, "I think that you should at least give Jackson's two thousand back to him."

"Would Matt Crow, his own brother, have given Jackson's money back if he'd won? Hell, no. And neither am I. Besides, I'll need it if I'm going to play poker with these guys. The stakes are steep."

"*Poker?* You're going to play *poker* with all that money? I don't believe this."

"You object to poker?"

"No, not if you can afford to play. If it were penny-ante and the pots weren't over a dollar, fine, but, Kyle, these men are all millionaires. To them a hundred dollars is like a penny to you or me. You'd be in over your head. I think that you should put that money in the bank. Maybe Noah could give you some pointers about investing it. He's into banking and seems like a very nice man.''

Kyle's eyes narrowed. "I don't think he's so nice. He seems kind of shifty-eyed to me. I'll bet he's a crook.''

"Oh, Kyle, surely not.''

"I wouldn't be surprised. I'll do some nosing around. And you'd better watch out for Spud Hall. Not only is he a little rough around the edges, but I heard some talk that he's considering filing for Chapter Eleven.''

"You mean he's going bankrupt?''

"Damned near. I overheard him hitting up a couple of the men for a loan.''

"Oh, how sad. Kyle, if he needs money that badly, you certainly should give Spud back his thousand dollars. He shouldn't be gambling on such a silly thing when his livelihood is in jeopardy.''

"No way. He's a proud man, and right now a thousand dollars is a drop in the bucket to him. He owes millions. And the word is that Carlton Gramercy is on shaky ground, too. Business has been down quite a while for companies that manufacture oilfield equipment.''

"Really?''

"Yep. Those two may have to turn in their membership cards any day now. And Mitch Harris—" Kyle cocked one eyebrow and shook his head.

Irish eased forward in her seat. "What about Mitch?"

"I hate to repeat it. It's just a rumor. Ah, here's the wine."

Her curiosity piqued, she tried to get Kyle to tell her what he'd heard about Mitch Harris, but no matter how much she wheedled, he would say no more. He changed the subject and became the perfect dinner companion: charming, entertaining, and solicitous.

As he told a witty story, Irish cupped her wineglass against her lower lip and absently ran her tongue along the rim as she watched him. The candlelight sparked his eyes with a luminous glow that mesmerized her. The warmth of his personality seemed to reach across the table with wispy fingers to caress her cheek and stroke her tummy.

As he spoke, those gorgeous eyes seemed fixated on her mouth, and his thumb rubbed the bowl of his spoon. Back and forth, slowly, sensually, he rubbed the hollow. She could almost feel the callused pad against her flesh. A flush of heat shot through her, and she squirmed in her chair.

She tore her gaze from his thumb and gulped a swallow of wine.

Dear heaven, the man was so handsome, so—so— sexy that it was sinful. Kyle had that special gift of making her feel as if she were the most beautiful and fascinating woman in the world. Not only had she always enjoyed his company, but also from their kiss, she sensed that lovemaking between them would be fantastic. They seemed to fit together like hand and glove. But—

She sighed.

Kyle had everything that she was looking for except one thing. Money.

Twelve thousand dollars wouldn't go very far in providing the security she was looking for. Besides, he'd probably lose most of it playing poker.

Wouldn't you know? Here she was in the midst of almost a dozen Texas millionaires, *eligible* millionaires who were fighting for her attention, and she had the hots for the only one without a decent bankroll.

Cool it, Irish! This was not the man for her. She was going for the brass ring—no, the gold ring. One with lots of diamonds on it.

She flashed Kyle a bright smile, pushed back her chair and stood. "Dinner was delightful. Now if you'll excuse me, I think I'll find Vernon for dessert and coffee."

"But we haven't had our entrée yet."

Irish looked down at her half-eaten salad. "Oh." She sat down quickly, feeling like an absolute fool.

"Nervous?" Kyle asked.

She glanced up quickly to see if he was smirking. He wasn't. Maybe he didn't realize that it was her reaction to him that was making her jittery. "Maybe a little. All these millionaires are a bit daunting."

"Relax," he said, reaching across and giving her hand a little squeeze. "These guys put on their pants one leg at a time, just like regular people. Although," he whispered as he began rubbing the valley between her thumb and forefinger with the same slow stroke as he used on the spoon, "I wouldn't let myself get caught alone with any of them just yet."

She jerked her hand away. "Why not?" she squeaked loudly. She cleared her throat and lowered her voice. "Why not?"

Kyle raised his eyebrows and gave an innocent-looking shrug. "Remember that these men are a competitive bunch. I wouldn't be surprised if they got another bet going and—" He shrugged again.

Outraged, she leaned across and whispered hotly, "Do you mean that—that they have a bet about who can score with me first?"

"Now, I didn't say that, honey."

"You intimated it!"

"Just forget that I brought it up. I'm sure that you don't have a thing to worry about. I haven't heard about any kind of pot like that. Ah, here's our fish."

Irish couldn't forget about it. Her stomach was in such a knot that she barely touched her food. She ate a few bites, then pushed the rest around on her plate.

Dessert with Spud was uneventful. Thankfully, he didn't try to entice her to his room or into a nearby broom closet. Between stuffing his face with pecan pie, mostly he talked about the bridge he was building and the Dallas Cowboys. He was a nice enough man, but too rough around the edges for her, even if he wasn't filing for bankruptcy.

Now Noah Birchfield, one of the few men who didn't seem to wear cowboy boots all the time, was a different matter. The banker, his manner suave and urbane, led her to a secluded table on a side porch where a candle flickered inside a crystal globe. Champagne was chilling in a silver bucket, and on the white tablecloth, dishes of cheese and chocolate-dipped strawberries waited beneath glass domes.

"How lovely," Irish said as Noah held out a chair for her.

"Not half as lovely as you, my dear."

She felt herself go warm as he bowed and brought her hand to his lips in a gracious, courtly gesture.

Candlelight glinted off his scalp as he nibbled her fingers. His manners weren't the only thing that was the epitome of polish. But, hey, what was a little male pattern baldness when one could offset the deficit with oodles of cash? Besides, there were always hair-weaves.

"Playing Peeping Tom?"

Kyle startled at Jackson's words and glanced away from the window. "They're on their third glass of champagne, and the bastard's hand-feeding her strawberries."

"That Noah is a smooth operator. He doesn't let any grass grow under his feet. I don't know what he's got, but I understand that the ladies are crazy about Noah. He seems right smitten with our Miss Ellison.''

"Dammit, she's *mine!*"

"Maybe you should tell her that. She looks quite taken with Noah. By the way, you owe me twelve thousand dollars and a kiss.''

Kyle scowled. "What are you talking about? I don't owe you anything, and I'm sure as hell not about to kiss you.''

Jackson chuckled. "I'm not too thrilled with the notion, either. Who's the luckiest man you know?''

Kyle didn't have to think about that one. Jackson was. Always had been. Even when Grandpa Pete gave each of his grandchildren a million dollars as a graduation present, promising to up it to ten if the recipient could double the million in two years, Jackson had depended on his lucky streak. Instead of investing the money or starting a business and working his butt off like the rest of them, Jackson had bought lottery tickets with most of his million.

And damned if he hadn't won. Eleven million dollars.

"What does your being lucky have to do with me kissing you?''

"To tell the truth, cuz, I'm more interested in the cash from you. Now I wouldn't mind a kiss from our lovely Miss Ellison.''

"Like hell!''

"Whose name do you think Irish pulled out of that hat?''

Kyle frowned. "Not mine?"

"Nope. I cheated a little when she asked me to read it. Wonder where they're going?" Jackson asked, craning his neck to peer through the window.

"Let me see." Kyle elbowed his cousin aside to get a better look. "Where did they go?"

"Down the path toward the fish pond."

"If he touches her, I'll break his legs."

Jackson widened his eyes in mock astonishment. "And you a doctor? What about your Hippocratic oath?"

"He's not my patient. I'll break his legs." Kyle turned and stalked off toward the side door while Jackson chuckled behind him.

Irish realized too late that taking a walk with Noah to see the fish was a bad idea. Not only was it too dark to see any carp in the murky shadows of the lily pads but also she realized that Noah shouldn't have had that last glass of champagne. He'd obviously hoisted a few before their tête-à-tête began. His courtly behavior had slipped a couple of notches.

The man was blotto.

When his hand slid from her waist down to cup her bottom, she grabbed his fingers and danced away. "Uh, uh, uh," she said, trying to keep it light. "None of that, Mr. Birchfield."

"Noah, sugarbabe. Call me Noah." He lunged toward her and got her penned between the bridge railing and him. "I've been wanting a taste of those luscious lips ever since I first laid eyes on you. Come on, give us a kiss.''

She tried to twist away, but he planted a sloppy kiss on her chin and started nuzzling her throat. Panic began to build inside her. *Stay cool, stay cool.* She could handle this, she told herself. The man was drunk and overly amorous. She'd dealt with situations like this before.

Irish tucked her chin and squinched her shoulder to deny him access to her neck and tried to push him away. "Mr. Birchfield—"

"Noah."

"Uh, Noah, please stop this. You've had a little too much to drink, and you don't know what you're doing."

His chuckle raised the hairs on the back of her neck. "Oh, I know all right. I'm doing what's been on both our minds since I fed you that first strawberry."

What a fool she'd been to flirt with him! His grip tightened, and he sought her mouth again.

With familiar hysteria clawing at her chest, she twisted and thrashed her head, trying to escape his hold. "Let me go. Please, let me go."

He thrust his knee between her legs, his hand down her blouse. The fabric ripped, a deluge of horrifying memories flooded her awareness, and she lost it. Her scream slashed through the night.

"You bastard!" an angry voice roared. Suddenly she was free, but she couldn't stop screaming.

A crunch, a splash, then another's arms were around

her. The familiar masculine scent penetrated her terror, enveloped her, comforted her.

Her trembling fingers clutched his shirt. "Kyle?"

"Yes, darlin', it's me. Calm down. It's okay."

"Kyle, I—he—"

"Shhhh. It's okay."

"What's going on?" Jackson asked as he ran up.

Kyle kept his arms around Irish and his hands stroking her back. "You might want to drag Birchfield out of the pond before he drowns, but I'm telling you now, if I ever see the son of a bitch again, I may kill him."

"To hell with Birchfield," Jackson said. "Is she all right?"

"Physically? I think so, but emotionally she's a wreck."

"Do I need to call a doctor?"

"Dammit, Jackson!"

"Oh, yeah. I forgot. Listen, why don't you take her into that cabin over there until she calms down. It's empty and unlocked. I'll deal with Noah."

Kyle swung Irish into his arms and strode to the nearby cabin. She clung to his neck like a child, her head burrowed against his chest. Her whole body quivered as if she were freezing.

He carried her inside, turned on a lamp and sat down on the couch with her still clinging to him. Her teeth chattered as she tried to speak.

"Shhhh, darlin'. It's okay. Are you cold?"

She nodded her head vigorously.

"Shall I light the fire?"

She nodded again. When he started to lift her aside and rise, she whimpered and her grip tightened around his neck.

He touched his lips to her forehead. "Sweetheart, I can't hold you and light the fire both."

"Forget the fire. Just hold me. Hold me tight. Don't let me go. I was scared, so scared. It brought back memories. Awful memories of the man—the man in New York. He broke into my apartment and tried— and tried to rape me. I fought and he cut me." She sucked in a shuddering breath. "He cut my face. I screamed and screamed. Hold me, Kyle. Hold me and keep me safe."

"Shhhh. I'll keep you safe. I won't let you go." With one hand he grabbed a woven throw tossed over the back of the couch, spread it around her and tucked in the edges. He chafed her arms and brushed his lips against her temple.

For the longest time he simply held her, not speaking, not moving. The only sounds in the room were his breathing and hers and the tick of a mantel clock. After a while her shivering lessened, then stilled.

"He didn't rape me. He ran away. They never caught him. A plastic surgeon fixed my face, and a psychologist fixed my head, and I'm just fine now. Just fine."

"You certainly are."

"I really am. Just fine.

"Almost."

He hugged her closer, his heart hurting from understanding the depth of pain she had endured and the phantoms that must continue to plague her. Frustrated that he could do no more than hold her, he would have kept her in his arms forever.

Slowly the tension that had drawn her muscles taut began to dissipate, and he could feel her relaxing against him.

She sighed deeply. "God, I feel like such an idiot."

He brushed a curl off her forehead and scanned her face. "Funny, you don't look like an idiot."

"What do I look like?"

"You look like a beautiful woman who has been badly frightened by an insensitive jackass."

She smiled and tucked her head under his chin. "He started out to be rather charming, but he was drunk."

"No excuse."

"I handled the situation badly. I overreacted. But all of a sudden I started having flashbacks, and I panicked."

"Even so, I heard you tell Birchfield to let you go. He didn't. Don't try to take the blame for his being a jerk. None of this is your fault. I'd like to castrate the scumbag with dull hedge clippers. I'd—"

Irish touched her fingers to his lips and smiled. "Now who's overreacting?"

He started to say more, but the words stuck in his throat. Their eyes met, and a spark flared between them. He ached to kiss her, but he recognized her vulnerability. No way would he indulge himself at her expense.

Besides, the way he felt, a kiss might not be enough. No, now wasn't the time.

"What are you thinking?" she murmured.

"Nothing."

"Liar." Her gaze dropped to his lips. He saw the pulse throbbing along her throat and heard her breath catch. "I owe you a kiss."

"You do?"

"Yes, for winning the pot."

His mouth began to move toward hers and hers to his as if they were drawn by magnets. Kyle checked himself. "Irish, I don't think—"

"Right. Don't think. Just kiss me."

Ten

Kyle didn't have to be told twice. His mouth captured hers, and Irish met his fervor with an intensity of her own. She shouldn't be doing this she told herself as she pulled him closer and touched her tongue to his, but it felt so absolutely heavenly.

The pressure of their lips increased, their breathing quickened, their tongues thrust wildly. He broke away and began frantically nuzzling her neck. "Irish, honey," he said between nuzzles, "we shouldn't be doing this now."

"Right," she said, throwing her head back to allow him greater access, "and don't get the wrong idea. This doesn't mean a thing."

"I know, darlin'." His tongue traced the length of her throat to the hollow at its base.

"I just need comforting," she said.

"I know, darlin'." He removed the gold chain and Texas pendant from around her neck and dropped it on the coffee table.

Uttering a sighing moan, she threaded her fingers through his wonderfully thick hair and urged him downward. When his tongue encountered a button, she scrambled to loosen it. And the one lower. And the rest. Anything to prolong the pleasure.

His tongue was magic, trailing chill bumps as it slid along the swell of her breast. Her nipple constricted and the sensitive flesh seemed to beg for his mouth.

"Kyle, please," she said breathlessly, urging his head downward.

"Please what, love?"

"Touch me. Take me in your mouth."

When he unhooked her bra and pushed it aside, a gold doubloon fell to the floor and rolled away. He touched the tip of his tongue to her nipple. "Here?"

"Yes. Oh, yes."

His lips closed around her and sucked. She squealed and almost went through the roof.

"Is that comforting?" he murmured.

"Unbelievably." She arched against him. "Comfort me some more."

And he did. Gloriously, expertly. Somehow in the comforting, all her clothes ended up on the floor, as did his. There wasn't a place on her body that he didn't taste or touch. Her skin became a thousand times more sensitive in the wake of his fingers, his lips, his tongue.

By the time he'd drawn a damp trail up her inner thigh, she was a seething mass of desire beyond anything she'd ever experienced. She grabbed fistfuls of his hair. "Kyle, oh Kyle."

"What do you want, sweetheart?" He blew gently against the wet place he'd made, and she sucked in a quick gasp.

"You. Inside me. *Now*."

"Are you sure, Irish?"

"Lord, yes!"

"You're not still sore from your horseback ride?"

"What horseback ride?"

"The one with Jackson that left you limping."

"I'm fine."

She didn't think she could get any more aroused, but he kissed her again and caressed her so thoroughly and so intimately that she was writhing and whimpering for him, urging him to her.

He moved between her legs and was about to enter when he stopped and cursed.

"What's wrong?" she moaned.

"Protection."

She stiffened. "Don't you have anything?"

"Hell, I hope so." He grabbed his pants from the heap on the floor and began rummaging through pockets. He cursed some more. "I don't suppose that you're on the pill?"

"Nope. Nor do I have any condoms with me. It didn't occur to me that I would need them."

Another round of cursing. "Wait right here," he said. "Don't move."

"Where are you going?"

"To the bathroom. I'm praying that this cottage is well stocked with every convenience."

It was. And before she could cool down and consider what was about to happen, he was back, kissing her again, murmuring lovely words, driving her wild.

When he entered her, she felt as if she had been waiting her whole life for that precise moment. She flung herself against him, and together they began the rhythmic, primal dance in perfect synchronization.

No place, no moment existed other than this. Raw sensation filled her and obliterated all thought as they moved and thrust and strove together. Each second lasted an eternity, and exquisite agony drove them on and on, reaching, seeking, demanding release.

Their frenzied movements tumbled them from the couch to the floor, but their fervor merely increased in questing tongues and kneading hands and urging moans. As the moment of her climax approached, he spoke provocative love words over and over, and her cries and her movements increased mindlessly.

"Yes!" she sobbed as the wave of sensation broke over her, convulsed her, bowed her back, and sent her awash with spasms of exquisite bliss.

Kyle cried her name and joined her in the surging sea of satisfaction.

For a long time they lay there, still joined, savoring the afterglow of lovemaking more profound than she could have imagined possible.

As they drifted back to reality, she discovered that she was lying on a shoe, and something sharp was gouging her bottom. Kyle's body became enormously heavy. She squirmed.

He lifted his head from her chest, kissed each breast, then chuckled as he shifted his weight off her. "How did we end up on the floor?"

"Search me."

He gave a devilish grin. "I'm game." His hands began exploring some very delicate places.

She squealed. "Kyle!"

"You don't like that? Doesn't it feel good?"

"Well, yes, but—"

He closed his lips around a nipple, and she sighed deeply.

"Do you like that?" he asked.

"What's not to like? But—"

His mouth moved to the opposite breast, and she forgot what she was going to say. Her nerve endings were at attention, but her brain was microwaved mush.

"Do you feel comforted?"

"Comforted?"

"I can see that I have my work cut out for me." He grinned, then picked her up, carried her to the bedroom and comforted her all night long.

A stream of sunlight flowed through a slit in the curtains. Irish's eyes opened with a start. She felt the weight of Kyle's arm across her waist and his breath against her shoulder.

Sudden anxiety tripped her heart. Dear Lord, had she—had they—

They had. Several times.

And it had been fantastic.

Had she gone mad? What had possessed her? She was scouting for a rich husband, not looking for a wild romp between the sheets with a penniless hunk.

She sighed. It had been wild. And wonderful.

But Kyle Rutledge was not the man for her. No. Absolutely not.

She had a vague memory of his telling her that he loved her. Had she dreamed it? No, she remembered hearing the words several times during their steamy night. Had she told him the same thing?

No. Surely not.

She couldn't love Kyle. It didn't fit in with her strategy at all. But she had a niggling feeling that she'd said something silly like that.

Irish shook her head vigorously, denying the possibility.

Kyle roused. He lifted his head, smiled and pulled her to him. "Good morning, darlin'. I hope you're not sore." He kissed her sweetly, then trailed his tongue along the curve of her ear.

"Not at all." Quickly she scrambled away from him and from the big bed, dragging a sheet with her and

wrapping it around her body. "I have to get dressed
and go. I have a breakfast date with Jackson."

He rolled over and stretched out on his side with
his head propped on his hand. He lay there gloriously,
unabashedly naked, a small smile playing around his
mouth as if he were amused. "We could have breakfast in bed instead."

"Oh, no. You're not going to divert me from my
plans. You know very well why I'm here. Now, I'll
admit that last night was nice—"

He raised one eyebrow. "Nice?"

"Nice. Very nice. But it didn't mean a thing."

His smile widened.

"Wipe that grin off your face, Kyle Rutledge. It
didn't mean anything, I tell you. I was upset, and you
comforted me. And I appreciate it. I really do, but
that's all it was. And if I said some ridiculous things,
they were just pillow talk."

"Pillow talk?"

"Yes, things one might say in the heat of the moment. In the morning those words mean nothing. Do
you understand?"

His eyes captured hers, and the intensity of his gaze
made her knees go weak. "I meant every word I said,
love."

Heat flooded her, and she felt her face flush. "Well,
I didn't. I don't think. I mean, well, I don't remember
exactly what I said. But I am grateful to you, Kyle. I
was very distressed, panicked, actually. Even if Noah
hadn't done what he did, I get that way sometimes,

especially at night. My therapist says that the feelings will go away when I regain my sense of safety and security.''

Kyle nodded solemnly. "I see. And you figure that a few million bucks will help?"

"Exactly. That few million that you disdain will buy lots of security. High fences, alarm systems, guard dogs—whatever is necessary. But more that than, lots of money will make me feel secure in here." She patted her chest.

He nodded again.

Holy cow! Why didn't the man cover himself? Here she was trying to explain to him why they couldn't get involved, why they were all wrong together, and he was lying there totally naked. Beautifully tanned. Muscular.

And growing aroused.

Her eyes widened.

His hand moved. "Need some more comforting?"

She dragged her gaze from the engorged area, clutched the sheet more tightly around her and jacked up her chin. "Certainly not! Have you no shame?"

He burst into laughter. "Not a bit."

Irish whirled and dashed for the bathroom.

She turned the shower on full force and stepped into the stall. She even considered turning the water to cold to quash the heat inside her, but she wasn't into masochism. With her face turned up to the pelting spray, she began furiously scrubbing with the soap bar.

The door opened, and Kyle stepped in.

"What are you doing in here?" she demanded, turning her back to him.

"Taking a shower." He plucked the soap from her fingers and began to lather her gently.

"Kyle?"

"Hmmmm?" he responded as he nibbled her shoulder and drew the soap between her legs.

"You shouldn't be doing that," she said as she leaned back against his chest.

"I shouldn't?" His hand replaced the soap.

"No, and I want you to stop." She sighed. "In a minute."

"I will, darlin'. In a minute."

"Kyle, this doesn't mean...a thing. We may have had a sexually exciting interlude, but I'm going to— a little higher...*ahhhh*...fantastic—I'm going to marry a millionaire. I have my heart set on it."

"I know, darlin'. I know."

Wearing her rumpled and torn clothes, Irish managed to dash across the grounds and get to her suite without being seen. She quickly changed into cotton slacks and a teal string sweater, slapped on makeup, then dashed back downstairs to have breakfast with Jackson.

She was fifteen minutes late, but he had graciously waited and stood when he saw her approach. He held her chair and signaled for a waiter to bring coffee and juice.

After she'd had a couple of jolts of caffeine, she

smiled at her host and said, "I apologize for being late."

"No problem. To tell you the truth, I wouldn't have been surprised if you'd stood me up. I'm really sorry about what happened with Noah. I don't know what got into the man except that he must have had too much to drink. In any case, a couple of the guys helped me dump him into a car, and I had one of the hands drive him to Dallas last night. He won't be back to bother you again."

"I'm sorry, too. I feel that my presence caused a problem."

"No, ma'am. Don't you think that for one minute. I don't want you to get the idea that his behavior is typical of Texas gentlemen. We don't need his kind fouling up the place. Hell, I think he was originally from Rhode Island or one of those little bitty Yankee states anyway. How about some breakfast?"

Jackson couldn't have been nicer or more gracious. And the man was drop-dead gorgeous, the epitome of tall, dark and handsome. But as they ate and talked, she thought how much more handsome he would be if his hair were blond instead of black and if his eyes were blue instead of brown.

While he was everything any woman could want, there simply wasn't that special something between them, that edge of sensual awareness that zinged over the skin and electrified the atmosphere.

But that could come with a little more time, she told

herself. A few kisses from that sexy mouth of his, and she'd probably be airborne.

As she watched him cut a slice of ham on his plate, she noted his large hands and long fingers. They reminded her of another pair of hands with wonderful, nimble fingers, and her mind wandered.

"Don't you think so?" Jackson asked.

She startled. "I beg your pardon?"

"I said that after your bad experience with Noah that we probably ought to forget about scheduling your time with the rest of the bunch."

"Oh, no. Not at all. I'm okay. I just won't go walking down any dark paths with anybody."

"Irish, I can assure you that you won't have any more trouble here. Word has gotten around about Noah, and the rest of the guys are pretty riled up about it. We don't want you to think badly of Texas men because of one snake."

"I won't. I promise."

Remembering that whatever happened, she had a commitment to *Esprit,* she fished her notebook from her bag and asked Jackson several questions that she thought readers would be interested in.

When they had finished the interview and the meal, Jackson located the hat with the business cards in it, and together they made out the schedule for lunches, cocktails and dinners. After-dinner times were left free, and she breathed easier about that. She could join the group or spend extra time with Jackson or any of the others that struck her fancy.

"You play golf?" Jackson asked.

"I don't know a putter from an iron."

He laughed. "That's been said of me from time to time. We're playing eighteen holes this morning. You can either ride in one of the carts with us or you can laze around the pool until lunchtime."

Knowing that she would cramp the style of the golfers, she opted for the pool.

Irish didn't realize that she'd dozed on the chaise for so long until a hand touched her shoulder and shook her gently. She jerked awake, the habitual panic seizing her until she became aware of where she was.

Carlton Gramercy, still in his golf clothes, stood beside her. He smiled. "Sorry to startle you, but I believe that I won lunch. Would you like to eat here by the pool?"

"That would be great."

"I wouldn't mind a dip to cool off," he said. "I'll go change and have our food delivered here. Any preferences?"

"Anything is fine, thanks."

After Carlton left, Irish grabbed her purse and began hurriedly repairing her makeup. While Carlton wasn't nearly as handsome as Jackson, he was nevertheless a very attractive man. And even though Kyle had said that his business might be on shaky ground, she didn't know that for a fact. He was a possibility, definitely a possibility.

Just as she snapped her compact, she heard a splash

and glanced up to see someone swimming underwater toward her. Carlton was certainly quick.

Near her, a head emerged from the pool. Not Carlton's. Kyle's.

He hung on to the apron and grinned through the water trickling down his face. "Hi, there. The water's great. Come on in."

"No, thank you. Carlton and I are about to have lunch. I don't want to get my hair wet."

"I've seen you with your hair wet, and I thought you looked sexy."

"*Kyle!* Shhhh." She glanced over her shoulder to see if anyone had overheard them. Not another soul was around. "Go away."

"I think I'll hang around and swim for a while. It was hot on the golf course. Did I tell you that I shot a seventy-eight? Not bad, if I do say so myself. I won another twenty-two hundred dollars."

"That's very nice. Now scram. Carlton will return any minute."

"If I were you, I'd put on that robe. After all, not only is Carlton's business going down the tubes, but he has two kids and a live-in lady friend in Lubbock. You wouldn't want to give him any ideas."

"Buzz off, Kyle. I don't believe half of what you say."

"Would I lie to you?" He smiled. "If you'll recall, I told you that Birchfield was shifty-eyed and couldn't be trusted. Put on the robe."

"Oh, very well." She grabbed the sheer cover-up

and pulled it on. "Now would you please paddle away?"

"Your wish is my command." With a splash, he was gone.

Carlton returned, and their food arrived a few minutes later. Dark-haired with touches of gray beginning at the temples, he looked very nice in a bathing suit—except for the little bit of a basketball tummy, which was nothing she told herself.

He was almost as charming as Jackson, and while they chatted over lunch, he made no mention of a significant other or two kids, nor did he give any indication that his business was having problems. She asked a few pointed questions and tried to take notes for her article, but she kept being distracted. Every time she glanced up, Kyle was shaking his head and making thumbs-down signals.

Dinner with Mac was almost as disastrous—not because of Mac, but because of Kyle. As she and Mac, a leather-skinned man with sun-bleached sandy hair, lingered in a dining alcove after their meal, talking about finding ocean treasure and listening to taped music, Kyle strolled up bold as brass.

"I believe that this tango is ours," Kyle said. Before she could do more than sputter, he pulled her up and into his arms. "You do tango, don't you?"

"Of course I tango, but—"

"I was sure that you could. You were born for the tango." He pressed his cheek to hers and slunk across the small dance floor. Every time she tried to protest, he spun her out like a yo-yo, brought her back with a thump against his chest and slunk to the opposite side of the floor in what had become a parody of Morticia and Gomez.

"Dammit, Kyle—"

He dipped deeply and draped her over his arm. "God, you're sexy when you dance."

"Kyle Rutledge—"

"I love the way you cry my name." He twirled her out, then back, yanked her hard against him, and headed across the room again.

Thankfully the song finally ended. When she tried to pull away and return to Mac, Kyle held her fast. "Wait. Listen. That's a samba. Do you samba?"

"Yes, I— No. No, I don't samba."

He grinned. "Too late, I caught you." He began a spirited, hip-swinging, one-two-three back and forth.

Irish struggled from his arms. "Listen, Desi Arnez, if you want to samba, do it by yourself. I have a date, remember?"

"Ah, yes. With the jailbird. Has he told you about the time he spent in the pokey?"

She turned and stalked away. Mac rose as she returned to the table. "Sorry," she said as he held her chair.

"I'm sorry, too," Kyle added. He grabbed a chair, turned it and straddled it backward. "I've been itching to talk with you some more, Mac, and ask you some questions about that galleon you found off the coast of Puerto Rico two years ago."

Irish could have gleefully wrung his neck. Despite her hints, Kyle stuck around like a barnacle to an old ship.

When she finally conceded defeat and said goodnight to Mac, Kyle rose and smiled. "I'll walk you to your door." He winked at Mac and said, "She and I are neighbors, you know."

All the way up the elevator, Irish ground her teeth to keep from yelling at him. If Kyle thought he was going to spend the night in *her* bed, he was badly mistaken.

Eleven

Irish slowly opened one eye, spied the blond head on the pillow next to hers and groaned. How had she allowed it to happen again?

It was the kiss that did it.

"Just one little good-night kiss," he'd said. "No harm in that."

No harm. And she'd fallen for it.

Well, no more.

She whacked him on the bare butt. "Kyle, get up. Go to your own room before someone discovers you here. And this is the absolute last time you're getting into my bed. I don't know why I ever let you inside the door. I must be mad. You're not my type. Not my type at all."

"Because I'm not rolling in dough? You didn't seem to mind that last night." He grinned. "As a matter of fact, I seem to remember your saying—"

"Nothing. I said nothing of any consequence. Mere pillow talk. Nothing to be taken seriously."

"Some of it sounded very serious to me. Oh, Kyle, baby," he mimicked in a falsetto voice, "you're the only man for me. I could never love—"

Irish whacked him with a pillow. "Hush. I don't want to hear anything you have to say. It's all baloney. Aren't you supposed to tee off in twenty minutes?"

"What time is it?" He bolted upright and looked at the clock. "Oops. You're right. Jackson will have my head if I'm late." He gave her a quick peck and scrambled from her bed. Hurriedly he donned his pants and gathered the rest of his clothes in a bundle. "See you later, sugar."

"Not if I can help it. You stay away from me today," she yelled after him. "You're screwing up everything."

Irish fell back in bed and pulled the covers over her head. Why had she spent another night with him?

Dumb. Dumb. Dumb.

She'd never had any trouble telling a man, "No." She was an accomplished no-sayer and, frankly, never much of one for casual sex, especially with all the scary consequences. But something about Kyle was beyond her experience. She would simply have to strengthen her resolve. How could she expect to snag one of the Texas millionaires when she kept shacking up with another man?

Was spending nights with Kyle worth blowing the chance of a lifetime?

A memory from the night before flitted through her mind, and she sighed and smiled. It was a close call. Kyle was the most fantastic lover in the world. The way he—

No! By damn she wasn't going to let him interfere with her plans. She'd come to Texas to find a wealthy husband, and that's what she was going to do.

She threw aside the cover and marched to the dresser to find her list. Lunch was with Aaron Golden. He owned a chain of men's discount clothing stores, and the diamond pinky ring he wore was probably worth more than two years' salary for her.

Going to the closet, she flung open the door and surveyed the contents. She had the entire morning to get ready, and she planned to knock Aaron dead.

Aaron was already dead. Or near enough to it that nobody would notice the difference. She stifled a yawn as she pushed peas around her plate. Aaron the dandy was an insufferable bore. Where was Kyle when she needed him?

Cocktails with Jim Welborn wasn't much better. She couldn't seem to work up an interest in rice farming and grain storage. He was a truly nice man, but dull. Very dull. Excruciatingly dull. And he kept mentioning someone named Dixie. She wasn't sure if

Dixie was his dog or his lady love. Whichever was welcome to him.

Now Mitch Harris was another story. Mitch had made his money playing professional football, retired from the team three years before and spent his time managing his investments and breeding quarterhorses. He was a good-looking man with enormous shoulders and a boyish grin that crinkled the corners of his blue eyes. His hair was light brown, curly and just long enough to kick up a bit in the back.

During dinner Mitch was as smooth as a river stone. He was bright, personable and a wonderful conversationalist.

"I don't seem to get along well with horses," Irish said. "My first afternoon here I went riding with Jackson and got thrown twice."

Mitch winced. "Ouch. I've been thrown a few times myself, and it's no fun. But I'll bet that I'm a better teacher than Jackson. I'd be happy to put you on a gentle mount and give you lessons if you'd come visit my ranch."

"Where is your ranch?"

"Near a little town called Brenham. It's easy driving distance from Houston or Austin. I have several hundred acres there. It's a beautiful spread, and in the springtime, there's no place like it. The fields are a sea of blue from the wild bluebonnets. I'd love for you to see it, but I wouldn't want you to wait until spring to come. You have an open invitation. The sooner, the better."

"Sounds wonderful," Irish said, beaming her best smile.

Kyle came ambling up to their table. "How's it going, kids? Sorry to interrupt, but you have a phone call, Mitch. You can take it at the desk."

Mitch excused himself and hurried away. Kyle took Mitch's chair, glanced around, then leaned forward and whispered, "I didn't want to tell you this, but I think you should know so that you won't get your hopes up about Harris."

"What are you talking about?"

Kyle glanced around again. "He's gay."

"He is not!"

"Oh, but he is. A real swell fellow, but definitely gay."

"Kyle Rutledge, you're making that up. I don't believe you. He was a professional football player, for gosh sakes."

He shrugged. "There are lots of gay football players. Basketball and baseball players, too. Ask Jackson about Mitch if you don't believe me." He stood and strolled away.

When Mitch returned, he was as gracious as ever, but she kept scrutinizing him and wondering. She couldn't get the question of his sexual preference out of her head. Surely this wonderful, hulking specimen of manhood wasn't gay. If he was, what a waste.

But she'd bet anything that Kyle was lying.

Whether Mitch was or whether he wasn't, in any case, Kyle had effectively put a damper on the evening. She went upstairs early, locked her door, wedged a chair under the knob and went to bed. Alone.

After breakfast, the men stood en masse and left for the golf course. Irish waved goodbye and had another cup of coffee.

The place was quiet without the men around. She strolled to the front desk and chatted with Tami for a few minutes, then looked at her watch. She had three and a half hours to kill before her lunch with Bob Willis.

Going swimming didn't appeal to her, and she didn't have a partner for tennis. She wasn't in the mood for staying in her room and reading or watching TV. And she certainly didn't want to get on a horse.

Cherokee Pete.

She smiled. Of course. She'd love to see the old man.

"Well, I'll be switched," Pete said a half hour later when Irish showed up in his room. "Look who's here. You run along, Steve," he said to the nurse, "and let me visit with this pretty lady. Irish used to be one of them models like Cindy and Claudia, you know, but a right smart better looking than either one of them, if you ask me."

Irish laughed. "You old charmer. What are you reading?" She picked up the book on his bedside table. "A romance novel?"

"Yep. Told you I like to read purt near everything.

Steve isn't near as good a reader as you are, and to
tell you the truth, I think some parts of it, he's em-
barrassed to say out loud." Pete slapped the bed and
guffawed. "Bother you?"

"Not a bit. I love romances. Shall I read to you for
a while?"

"You betcha."

She read for over an hour, and they talked for a few
minutes longer, mostly about his wife. The romantic
story had made him sentimental.

"I was a rounder when I was a young man," Pete
said. "But the moment I met my Molly, I knew she
was the woman for me, and I never looked at another
one."

Irish lifted her brows. "Never?"

"Well, that is to say, I might have looked a little
once in a while, but that's all I did. I never had a
hankering for anyone but her. I fell hard and loved her
something fierce. I suspect that's the way my grandsons will be when they find the right woman. How
you and Kyle gettin' along?"

She smiled. "Still trying to match-make?"

"Yep. Kyle would skin me if he knew I'd offered
again, but I'm serious about that two million." His
dark eyes gleamed as he grinned at her. "I'd like to
keep you around."

"That's very sweet of you, but I don't think Kyle
is the one for me."

"You sure? I'd up my offer to ten for a little of
nothing."

Laughing, she stood and kissed his cheek. "Pete, you're a piece of work. I'm going downstairs for a package of Ding-Dongs. Want to half it with me?"

"I reckon. How about Jackson? You take a shine to him? Jackson's a good boy, a little wild sometimes, but no wilder'n—"

A broad-shouldered woman appeared in the doorway. "It's time for your therapy, Mr. Beamon."

"Go away, woman, you're only here to torture me. And can't you see I've got company? We're in the middle of serious negotiations."

"Don't go giving me any of your nonsense," the physical therapist said. "This is for your own good and you know it."

"She's a slave driver," Pete told Irish. "She could teach Simon Legree a thing or two."

Irish winked at him. "And so could you, I'll bet. I'd better go. I'll come again soon."

She went downstairs and visited with Alma Jane and Jenny for a few minutes, then bought a package of cupcakes. When she paid Jenny for them, she realized again how slim her pocketbook was. She had only a couple more days to land one of those millionaires or she was in deep trouble. Her charge card was maxed, and she didn't have enough cash to buy a tank of gas for the rented car.

If worse came to worst, she could probably borrow enough from Kyle to get back home, but she didn't intend for things to get that bad. She'd come to Texas to hook a millionaire, and by gosh, that's what she was going to do!

She had only to decide which one.

Jackson Crow still seemed the best prospect. She hadn't seen any evidence that he drank any more than anybody else. Or maybe Mitch Harris. She didn't believe for one minute that he was gay. She didn't hold out much hope that Bob Willis would be in the running nor Harve Dudley, her cocktail date.

Mac was a possibility. She could get used to tooling around on a yacht and running her fingers through piles of gold coins and antique jewels. And she shouldn't forget that Matt Crow had to be considered. He was a cutie-pie, and she was having dinner with him that night.

They might be perfect together. You never knew.

Irish freshened up and went down to meet Bob for lunch. Kyle was leaning against the wall when the elevator door opened.

"Hi, sugar," he said, breaking into a broad smile. "Ready for lunch?"

"Yes, I am, and please don't call me sugar. If you'll excuse me, I have a date with Bob Willis."

"Uh, well...no, you don't."

"Of course I do. It's on my schedule."

"There's been a slight change in the schedule."

"Oh?"

"Yes. Now you're having lunch with me." He offered his arm.

She ignored it. "And exactly how did that come about?"

"I won you."

"You *won* me?"

"Yep. On fourteen. He bogeyed, and I birdied. I won you."

"Let me get this straight. You and Bob Willis had a bet on the golf course—"

"On fourteen. It's a killer."

"And Bob gambled his lunch date with me? Against what?"

"Five thousand dollars."

Her eyes grew wide. "You bet *five thousand dollars* against a lunch date with me? Are you mad?"

"About you." He kissed her cheek. "I'm starved. Shall we go?" He offered his arm again.

Irish muttered all the way to the table. Five thousand dollars? She couldn't believe that Kyle would do such a stupid thing. Then she thought about the situation some more and became even more irritated.

Kyle glanced at her over his menu. "What's wrong, love?"

"Nothing is wrong. I'll have the cold salmon and the hearts of palm."

"Wine?"

"Tea."

"If nothing is wrong, why is your bottom lip drooping?"

She drew herself up straight. "It is *not* drooping."

She was quiet for a few minutes after Kyle ordered

their lunch, then when they were alone again, he said, "Want to tell me about it now?"

"If you must know, my pride is a little hurt that Bob gambled me away like a prize pig. I'm beginning to feel about as valuable as a poker chip."

"Oh, honey." He squeezed her hand and brought her fingers to his lips for a kiss. "Don't feel bad. I goaded him into it. Ask Carlton. Ask Harve. They were in my foursome. Anyway, Bob isn't a prospect. He's getting married in two weeks to a divorcée who owns the spread next to his." Kyle leaned forward and lowered his voice. "Trust me, you wouldn't have enjoyed his company. The man has bad breath like you wouldn't believe."

Irish burst into laughter. "Kyle Rutledge, you're as big a piece of work as your grandfather. I went to see him this morning. He seems to be doing fine, but he wasn't too excited about having to do his physical therapy."

"So I hear. I talked to him last night. But the therapy is doing wonders. Indications are that he'll be completely mobile in another week or two. The problem then will be trying to keep him from overdoing."

"He's such a sweetheart. This morning I read to him from a romance novel, and he upped his offer to ten million dollars if I'd marry you."

Kyle almost knocked over his glass, catching it as it teetered and sloshing water onto the cloth. "I hope you don't take the old man seriously," he said, drying his hand with his napkin.

"Oh, certainly not. And I told him that you weren't my type. Now I think he's touting Jackson as a candidate. That might not be a bad idea."

The glass toppled completely, flooding the tablecloth with water and ice and sending a cold stream into his lap. "Dammit!" Kyle shouted, leaping to his feet.

The waiter hurried over and contained the spill on the table as Kyle tried to mop his wet pants. Jackson ambled along behind, then stopped, looked pointedly at the wet stain across Kyle's fly and chuckled. "I've heard of cold showers, but I guess this is an effective substitute in a pinch."

"Dammit, Jackson," Kyle ground out as Irish tried not to laugh, "it's not funny."

"It is to me," he said, winking at Irish. "Why don't you go change your britches, and I'll entertain the lady while you're gone."

Kyle glowered. "I'm not leaving her alone with you."

"Man, what's gotten into you? Look around. There are a dozen people here. I assure you that she's perfectly safe with me. Go on."

"Oh, hell! I'll be right back." Kyle threw his soggy napkin on the table and stalked off.

"Shall we move to a dry table?" Jackson asked, still obviously amused. When they were resettled and the waiter had poured fresh water, he said, "What's gotten into that boy? I've never seen him act so goofy.

You must be the cause of it." He grinned knowingly. "Are things getting serious?"

"Oh, no," she said quickly. "Golly, no. Kyle is very nice, but he's not my type at all."

"He's not?" A slow grin lifted one side of his mouth as he reached for a newly poured glass of water. "What type do you prefer?"

She felt suddenly shy, but she gave herself a mental swift kick and said, *Go for it, babe. This may be your best chance.* Licking her lips, she leaned forward, rested her chin on her hands, gave him the dynamite smile that had graced the cover of *Glamour* and said in a breathy voice, "I like my men tall, dark and handsome." She let her long lashes sweep over him as she ran her toes up his leg. "Like you."

Over crashed Jackson's glass. He made a lunge for it, but only succeeded in knocking over Irish's glass, too. This time Irish got a lapful of ice and water as well as her table mate. She jumped up as the cold stream hit her.

"Dammit!" Jackson roared, leaping up to try to sop the water that had sloshed onto her clothes.

"What in the hell are you doing?" Kyle roared as he hurried up.

Jackson's hand froze as he dabbed the front of Irish's slacks. He looked at his hand, then up at Kyle. "You wouldn't believe it if I told you." To Irish he said, "Beg pardon, ma'am. I think it's our turn to change." He offered her his arm. "If you don't mind, Irish, I believe I'll have Curtis serve our lunch by the pool. We can put on bathing suits and save cleaning bills.''

"Nobody invited you to lunch, Jackson," Kyle said sharply. "Irish and I will have room service."

Irish discreetly poked Kyle with her elbow. "Oh, don't be such a goose. We'll all have lunch together by the pool." She gave Jackson another winsome smile.

Jackson grinned and winked.

Twelve

Kyle and Jackson stood in the hall outside Irish's door, waiting while she changed. Kyle scowled at his cousin. "You look ridiculous, Jackson. Who are you trying to kid in that getup?"

Jackson, who wore a black cowboy hat, a low-slung black bathing suit, a cropped Dallas Cowboys T-shirt, black boots and aviator glasses, glanced down at his attire. "What's ridiculous about it? You don't like the Cowboys?"

"You know damned well that I'm talking about your hat and wearing boots with those bare, hairy legs. You look like you're about to do a dance number in one of those beefcake places."

"Now there's something that I haven't tried." Jackson grinned. "The hat is to keep the sun off my head, and I like boots. Hell, I paid nearly fifteen hundred dollars for that custom-made pair I play golf in. These are my pool boots. See? Rubber soles." He lifted one foot to show the bottom. "And as for my hairy legs, do you think I ought to shave them?"

Kyle couldn't help but laugh and shake his head. "I swear, cuz, I don't think you'll ever grow up."

"I hope to hell not, especially if it means I'll have to wear Yuppie little deck shoes and coordinating swim wear. Kyle, good buddy, you spent too much time in California rubbing elbows with all those swishy designers. You always look real purdy and well put together, and I hate to tell you this, but I think your lady is more attracted to me than she is to you."

"The devil she is. Your bank account has temporarily dazzled her. She'll come around. Why don't you get lost now and let us have some time alone?"

"Nope. Irish invited me special, and I aim to please my guests. I just may decide to give you a run for the money with her. She's a very lovely lady. I like her."

Kyle opened his mouth to argue, but the door opened and Irish stepped out. She looked gorgeous in a green bikini with a matching sheer jacket.

"Sorry to be so long," she said, "but it's windy outside, and I took time to French-braid my hair." She touched the back that was caught up with a gathered bow.

"And may I say that it looks exquisite." Jackson swept off his hat and bowed.

"Thank you." She glanced down at Jackson's boots, then over to Kyle, her brows raised in surprise.

"Those are his pool boots," Kyle said.

He reached for her hand. Jackson offered his arm. "Shall we go?" they both said at the same time.

For a while, Irish reveled in the attention of two such handsome and virile males, but after an hour of it, she began to feel a bit like a lone cow standing on a hill while two bulls battled it out below.

She also got the feeling that Jackson wasn't taking the situation nearly as seriously as Kyle was, but then it was difficult to assume that anyone who wore boots with a bathing suit took anything seriously.

"I think our lunch has had time to settle," Jackson said to Irish. He stood. "Want to take a dip?"

"You go ahead," she said, "I'm going to wait a few minutes." Actually, she rarely went in the water. Because of her scars and her makeup.

"You going to wear your boots?" Kyle asked.

"In the pool? Man, are you crazy?" He yanked off his boots and set them aside, hung his hat on the back of his chair, and tossed his aviator glasses on the table.

Irish couldn't help but watch as he stripped the T-shirt over his head, his muscles rippling as he moved. He had a sensational body, deeply tanned with a dusting of dark chest hair that trailed down to the waistband of his skimpy suit in a particularly enticing way.

"Want me to start the music now?" Kyle muttered.

Jackson flashed him a white-toothed grin and

strolled to the high diving board. He climbed up, walked to the end of the board, winked at Irish and did a perfect half gainer into the water.

"Wonderful!" Irish clapped as Jackson broke the surface and breaststroked to the side.

"Oh, hell!" Kyle threw down his napkin, stood and stripped off the blue knit shirt that matched his purple, blue, and white patterned trunks. He kicked off his deck shoes and stalked to the board.

Kyle was no slouch in the physique department, either. His smoothly muscled chest was every bit as enticing as Jackson's. Maybe more.

Actually, some might say a lot more.

If you like the blond Adonis type with skin like golden honey.

His backward layout was beautiful.

Jackson got back on the board and did something a little fancier. Then Kyle matched it. Jackson did a somersault; Kyle did a somersault.

Mac strolled up, shaded his eyes and watched the action. "What's going on?" he asked Irish. "Olympic tryouts?"

"No. A pissing contest."

He chuckled. "I see. I have to drive into Tyler and autograph some books at one of the bookstores. Want to come along and keep me company? It shouldn't take more than a couple of hours, and I'll buy you an ice-cream sundae afterward."

"Make that a banana split, and you're on."

Mac smiled. "Yes, ma'am."

"Would you give me ten minutes to change clothes?"

"Oh, heck, I was hoping that you would wear your green bikini, and I could tell folks that you're a mermaid I found."

Laughing, she rose and the two of them headed for the lodge.

Winded, Kyle pulled himself onto the apron and swiped the water from his face. Jackson followed, shaking his wet head like a dog.

"Man, we're getting too old for this," Jackson said.

"I hear that. We're not sixteen anymore." Kyle glanced over his shoulder toward the table where Irish sat.

She was gone.

He scanned the pool area, but he didn't see anybody but Matt Crow and Spud sitting under one of the umbrellas carrying on a spirited conversation. "Where'd she go?"

Jackson shrugged. "Don't know."

He yelled at Matt, "Did you see Irish leave?"

"Yeah, she left with Mac a few minutes ago. They went back toward the lodge."

"Well, hell!"

"Don't worry about her," Jackson said. "Mac's a good man."

"That's what I'm afraid of. I've got to go find her." He scrambled to his feet, grabbed his shirt and took off for the lodge. He'd only made a few steps when he saw Mac and Irish drive away in a white BMW.

"Dammit!" Kyle slammed his shirt on the ground, then stood there dripping until the car was out of sight.

Jackson strolled up wearing his black hat and with a towel around his neck. An unlit cigar was clamped between his teeth. He threw his arm around his cousin and said, "Come on, hoss. Let's go hoist a cool brew and tell war stories. She'll be back."

"Jackson, I don't know what I'm going to do. She keeps me tied in knots most of the time. The rest of the time I want to beat my chest and do a Tarzan yell. I've never run into anything like this before. I feel like I'm going crazy."

"Sounds like love to me, cuz. I'd say that the best thing to do would be to either shoot yourself or marry her."

"I don't own a gun, and I'm afraid to ask her to marry me. I'm fairly sure that she would turn me down. I told you that she has her heart set on marrying a millionaire."

"Then, dammit, tell the woman the truth. Take it from somebody who's older and more experienced, every time you lie to a woman, you're digging yourself in deeper."

"Hell, Jackson, you're only three and a half months older than I am. Don't try to make yourself out a sage. And I'm in so deep now, it won't make any difference. I'm convinced that she's in love with me. But I just want her to admit it before she knows I'm as loaded as you are."

"Well, now I wouldn't go so far as to say that. How much you worth now, Kyle?"

"None of your damned business, but plenty. I sold my practice and property in California for a nice chunk of change."

"Don't let Spud hear you stay that. He'll try to rope you into his latest venture. Looks like he's got Matt cornered now. Let's go rescue my baby brother."

"Is Spud on shaky ground?" Kyle asked.

"Naw, he's got twice as much socked away as you and me put together. He just doesn't like to use his own money for some of his projects. Actually, I made a couple of million on one of his deals last year."

"How is Carlton Gramercy's business these days?"

"Going great guns. He's got a big contract with the Saudis, and they buy his oil field equipment as fast as he can manufacture it."

"Lord, I hope Irish doesn't find out about it."

"Why's that?" Jackson asked.

"Because I told her that Spud was about to file for Chapter Eleven and Carlton was barely making his payroll."

Jackson chuckled and shook his head. "I can see where you would be in deep dung about those tales. What else did you tell her?"

Kyle grinned. "That Mitch Harris was gay."

"Gay? *Mitch?*" Jackson threw back his head and roared with laughter.

* * *

Irish had thoroughly enjoyed her afternoon with Mac. One of the major bookstores in Tyler had quite a nice turnout, and he autographed fifty or so books in about an hour and a half. He tried to convince her that having such a beautiful woman along was the drawing card for several of the sales. She laughed and kissed him on the cheek for the compliment. Afterward, they went to a yogurt shop for their banana splits.

"I haven't had one of these in years," Mac said.

"Me, either. For so long I lived in such terror of gaining an extra ounce that I didn't even allow myself to think of such sinful treats."

"Why the concern for your weight? Were you a model or an actress?"

"A model. I worked in New York until I retired a couple of years ago."

Mac squinted at her and angled his head, first to the left, then the right. "Did you do that ad for the suntan lotion, the one in the fishtail and—"

"The seashells? Yep, that was me."

"No wonder I associated you with a mermaid. One of the divers kept that page taped to his locker aboard the *Which Witch* for a long time. Well, I'll be darned. That was you."

"That was me."

"Why did you retire? You're still a stunning woman."

"Thank you." Irish started to give him one of her

casual stock answers, but she glanced up and looked into his eyes.

He had the kindest, gentlest eyes that she'd seen in a long time. Something in his manner invited her to bare her soul to him. She looked down, dabbed her ice cream with her spoon, then proceeded to tell him the entire story of the attack and the agonizing months afterward, something she rarely talked about in detail. Why she chose someone who was almost a stranger to unload on, she didn't know.

It took her more than an hour, but she left nothing out—except the real reason for her trip to Texas and her intimacy with Kyle.

He laid his hand gently over hers. "You've had a tough time, haven't you?"

She shrugged. "Many have had it tougher. I made a good living as a model, and I had quite a bit of money saved and invested, but my insurance ran out, and my medical treatment took everything I had. I'm still in debt. My parents would help me if they knew, but my dad has a small butcher shop in Akron and my mom is a housewife. None of my family can afford to pay my bills. Aunt Katie leaving me her house in Washington was a godsend. With roommates, my job at the department store, and a few writing assignments, I get by. Not in the style that I used to, but I manage."

Mac squeezed her hand. "At the risk of sounding sexist, it seems to me like a gorgeous woman like you ought to snag a well-heeled husband from this gang gathered at Jackson's and live happily ever after."

She sighed. "That would be nice, wouldn't it? Truthfully the thought crossed my mind as well, but I don't think things are going to work out that way."

"You didn't find one that interested you?"

"Oh, but I did. Find one, I mean. But there are...complications." She stirred the last of the melted mush around in her dish. "I don't see it working out."

"I'm sorry. Would you let me help you? God knows, I've got more money than—"

"No. Oh, no. But that's very sweet of you, Mac, but I couldn't take anything from you." She didn't tell him that she still held out a slim hope that she and one of the millionaires would light a small spark. She wished that it could have been Mac. He was so sweet and so dear and lived such an exciting life that he was a perfect candidate, but there was nothing there. Not a whit of male/female attraction. And that was a shame, a real shame.

"I'll bet things work out with that special guy. You're a beautiful and authentic person, Irish. Any straight, single guy would be lucky to have you. Even I, if I were that kind of guy, would jump at the chance to be your love."

She glanced up. "You're married?"

He grinned. "No, I don't advertise the fact around the club—frankly, I keep very quiet about it—but I'm gay."

"You *are?* So's Mitch Harris."

"Mitch Harris?" Mac burst into laughter. "No, he's not. Believe me."

"Are you sure?"

"Positive."

Her eyes narrowed. "That rat! I may kill him."

Irish plotted revenge against Kyle all the way back to Crow's Nest, but she couldn't think of anything suitably dastardly. She finally tabled the notion and went upstairs to freshen up for her cocktail date with Harve Dudley, the Cadillac dealer who was engaged to Esther Ann. As a prospect, he was out of the running, but he was a colorful character for her article.

When she went downstairs to meet Harve, she found Kyle propped in his customary place by the elevator. She stuck her nose in the air, meaning to sail right past him, but he grabbed her as she went by.

"Where to in such a hurry?"

"I have a cocktail date with Harve, if it's any of your business."

He grinned. "Not anymore, you don't."

"What do you mean?"

"I'm substituting for Harve."

Furious, she shook off his grip. "I suppose that you won me on the golf course as well. Which hole was it this time?"

He winked. "No hole. This time I won you with a full house. Queens and fours."

"I'm surprised that you didn't challenge him to a diving contest."

"Are you miffed about that, honey? I'm sorry. Jackson and I fell into a childish pattern. We always competed as kids.''

Her nose went up another notch. ''I'm sure that I don't care what you and Jackson do.''

''Ah, honey, come on, don't be mad. I sweated bullets winning you from Harve. Let's have a drink.''

Suddenly a dastardly enough idea came to her. She turned to him and smiled sweetly. ''Very well. It's a lovely evening. Let's have a drink out on the porch.'' She let her fingers walk up his shirtfront. ''I'll have a frozen strawberry daiquiri. A double. Why don't you get our drinks from the bar, and I'll meet you outside.''

He bent and kissed her cheek. ''I'll be there in a flash.''

When he came out with the drinks a few minutes later, Irish was waiting in the shadows beside the porch railing. ''I'm here,'' she said breathily when he looked around.

He handed her the frozen daiquiri. ''Moonlight becomes you.''

''Thanks, but I've heard that before. A song, isn't it? Anyway, the moon isn't up yet, that's the vapor light.''

He smiled. ''The vapor light becomes you.''

He bent to nuzzle her neck, but she danced away. ''Kyle?''

''Yes, love?''

''I think Mitch Harris is an utterly charming man.

Did you know that he has invited me to visit his ranch?"

"Oh, really?"

"Yes." She walked her fingers down the front of his shirt to the waistband of his slacks. "Are you absolutely sure that he's gay?"

"Oh, yes. Absolutely sure. Forget about visiting his ranch. You shouldn't fritter away your time on him."

She yanked out his waistband and dumped the daiquiri down the front of his designer pants. "Liar!" She shoved in the glass as well, whirled, and marched off.

Kyle retrieved the glass, but he couldn't do much about the strawberry slush sliding from his crotch down his legs except endure it until it had run its course.

Things could have been worse. He could have been wearing tight jeans. Or Jackson could have witnessed this latest indignity. His cousin would have carried him high and ribbed him for the rest of his life. Thank God for small miracles.

Kyle heard a low chuckle from the end of the porch and withdrew his premature thanks. It was Jackson. Or Matt.

It turned out to be both. The brothers strolled up and looked him over. "Bet that's cold," Matt said.

"What is it with you and drinks in your pants?" Jackson asked. "Some kind of fetish?"

"Don't say another word, fellows, not another friggin' word," Kyle said sharply.

Matt pantomimed locking his lips, but Jackson grinned and said, "Told you that your lies were gonna catch up with you. You'd better tell that little lady the truth or you're gonna lose her for sure."

Kyle hung his head. "I guess you're right. I'll tell her tonight."

"If she'll still speak to you."

"If she'll still speak to me. Matt, how about letting me have your turn at dinner with her?"

"No, I don't think so."

"Dammit, Matt, name your price."

Thirteen

Irish couldn't have asked for a more delightful dinner companion than Matt Crow. With his dark hair and eyes, he was every bit as handsome as his older brother, maybe more so if one took the chin dimple into account. The air around him seemed to sparkle with his exuberance.

"More wine?" he asked, lifting the bottle.

"No more for me, thanks, but please have another glass yourself."

"One's about my limit. Two occasionally. I'm not much of a drinker."

Her ears perked up. So he didn't have Jackson's problem with alcohol. Interesting. Things were looking up. She realized now that perhaps she hadn't paid enough attention to Matt Crow. Tall, dark, handsome, rich.

Sober. Perhaps she'd found the best last.

Leaning forward, she rested her chin on the back of her hands and gave him a dazzling smile. "Tell me more about your fudge factory. Exactly where is it?"

They talked about fudge. They talked about Texas, the first time he soloed in a plane, her first runway job when she almost fell off the stage. She told him funny stories about life in New York; he told her funny stories about life in Dallas. She couldn't remember laughing so much in ages. All in all, their dinner was a smashing success.

Except for one thing.

Kyle sat across the room and glared at Matt the entire evening.

Irish tried to ignore Kyle's scowls, but she soon grew so uncomfortable that she suggested coffee on the porch.

The moon was up for real; the night was balmy and redolent with the crisp scent of pines and the faint fragrance of a scattering of late-blooming roses. After a few sips of coffee, Irish set her cup on the porch railing and leaned back against a post. Even with all the turmoil she'd experienced in the past few days, she couldn't recall feeling so...so light in years.

"I think I like Texas," she said.

"And Texans?" His cup joined hers.

She smiled. "And Texans. I've especially enjoyed our evening together. I like you, Matt Crow."

"Ah, shucks, ma'am. I kinda like you, too." He grinned at her without any pretense of toe-dragging shyness.

She chuckled. "You're a piece of work—in the very best sense."

"And you are an extraordinary woman—in the very best sense."

Her heart accelerated. Was it possible? Was he? Could they? She crossed her fingers and wished with all her heart. Then she licked her lips and said softly, "Matt, would you kiss me?"

He was quiet for a moment, as if caught off guard. "Why, sure. Of course." He kissed her very sweetly on the forehead.

"Not like that." She threw her arms around his neck, dragged his mouth close to hers and planted a good one on him.

She waited for bells to ring, fireworks to explode.

Nothing.

She increased the pressure of her lips on his, ground her body against him.

Nothing.

Not a tinkle or a tiny sizzle.

"Oh, no," she groaned, pulling away. "Oh, no. I'm sorry, Matt. I'm sorry." She turned and ran into the lodge.

Kyle called out to her as she ran by, but she didn't want to talk to him then of all times. The elevator closed before he could reach her, and it carried her upstairs to sanctuary.

She ran to her suite and hurriedly locked and bolted the door behind her. In a few seconds, Kyle was banging outside, calling her name. She didn't want to see him; she didn't want to talk to him. He'd ruined everything.

Scurrying to her bedroom, she closed and locked that door as well. Her back against the wood, she slowly slid down until she sat on the floor.

Damn him! He'd ruined everything.

Had she been captivated by Jackson Crow who owned oil wells out the kazoo or Matt Crow with his fudge factory and airline or Mitch Harris with his big bucks and big ranch? No? She hadn't been attracted to any of them, not Jim or Bob or Spud or Carlton or poor dull Aaron.

She'd fallen head over heels in love with Kyle Rutledge. *Kyle Rutledge!* And he was nothing but a poor chain saw sculptor.

How could she be so stupid?

Stripping off her clothes, she climbed into bed and tried to go to sleep.

She was wide-awake.

For almost an hour, she tossed and turned and tried to decide what to do. There was only one answer.

Having a mansion in Dallas and a butler and diamonds and a Beemer probably wasn't all it was cracked up to be anyhow. She was in love with Kyle. If they had to live in one of Pete's tepees for a while, she could survive. She'd survived worse.

Scrambling from the jumbled covers, she grabbed a

robe and ran to the door, determined to tell Kyle exactly how she felt about him. She loved him! Dammit, in spite of herself, she loved him.

Throwing open the door, she charged out into the hall, then stopped abruptly. Kyle sat on the floor, his knees drawn up and his head resting against the wall. He looked totally dejected, exhausted.

"Kyle?"

He glanced up.

She held out her hand. "Come to bed."

His smile was unbelievable. He was on his feet before she could draw another breath. He gathered her in his arms. "Oh, darlin', I love you so."

"I love you, too."

Pulling back, he scanned her face. "Say that again."

"I love you."

He hugged her so fiercely that she yelped. "Sorry, sweetheart, but you can't imagine how many times I've ached to hear you say that. Besides when we're in bed."

"I've never said it before! In bed or anywhere else." Her tone was indignant.

He laughed. "If you say so." Scooping her into his arms, he strode inside her suite and kicked the door closed. He began kissing her before he made it to the bedroom.

Bells clanged; fireworks burst in continuous explosions. The air sizzled with the electricity of their lovemaking.

It was a night that she would never forget.

* * *

Morning sunlight tickled Irish's nose and wakened her. She lay half atop Kyle, nude and in a tangle of covers. She touched her tongue to his nipple, and his eyes popped open.

"Good morning," she said.

"Good morning." He stroked her cheek and smiled. "Tell me again."

She laughed. "I must have told you a hundred times already. You'd better get up. It's the final day of the golf tournament."

"To hell with the golf tournament. Tell me again."

"I love you."

He hugged her close. "God, I love to hear you say that. I thought for sure that I was going to lose you to somebody else, one of the guys in the club. When I saw you kiss Matt last night, I must have died a thousand deaths."

"That's when I knew that I loved you. I kissed him and felt nothing."

"Matt's got a pile of money."

Irish sighed. "I know. I guess I'm not destined to marry a millionaire."

Kyle kissed her nose. "Yes, you are."

Her heart caught. He wasn't going to propose. Hesitantly, she asked, "What do you mean?"

"Honey, I have some things to tell you. Now, I want you to promise that you won't be angry with me. Promise?"

"How can I promise before I know what you mean?" She bolted upright. "Dear Lord, Kyle, are you married?"

"No, no, nothing like that. It's just that I haven't been entirely—uh, exactly forthright with you."

Her eyes narrowed. "And?"

He took a deep breath. "Well, I'm not just friends with Jackson and Matt. We're cousins."

"So?"

"There's more." He squirmed. "Uh, Pete has four grandsons and a granddaughter from his two daughters. My brother, Smith, and me—and Jackson and Matt and Ellen."

"Okay."

"Grandpa Pete doesn't need to run the trading post or carve cowboys and Indians and bears for a living. He's wealthy. I don't know how many millions of dollars he has."

Irish's jaw went slack. "*Pete? Our* dear old Cherokee Pete is a—a—"

"Millionaire. Rolling in dough. And the reason that Jackson and Matt and Ellen are rich is because when they graduated from college, Grandpa Pete gave each one of them a million dollars and a promise to up it to ten million if they could double their money in two years. They did."

"Wow." Slowly Kyle's tale began to sink in, and a sick feeling began building in the pit of her stomach. "If Pete gave each of his other grandchildren money, what about you and your brother?"

Kyle cleared his throat and glanced at the wall. "He did the same for Smith and me."

Stunned, Irish could only stare at him.

"He gave me a million after I—" he mumbled.

"Say again."

"He gave me my first million when I finished my residency."

"Your *first* million? Your *residency?*" she shrieked. "Your residency in what?"

He looked very sheepish. "Plastic surgery."

Fury flashed over her, and she leapt from the bed, dragging the sheet along for a toga. "You lied to me. Lied! You let me think that you were a penniless sculptor and Pete was a simple storekeeper, when all the time you're—you're—"

"Rich," Kyle supplied. "Honey, I'm sorry about that, but now you really can marry a millionaire. I'm loaded." He grinned.

Another realization came to her, and she grew horrified. "Who else was in on this charade? Jackson? Matt?"

He looked very uncomfortable. "Love—"

"They were. Oh dear God, how humiliating." Blood drained from her face when she realized that she'd been made a fool of and had been, no doubt, the butt of countless jokes around Crow's Nest. She'd thrown herself at Jackson and kissed poor Matt senseless.

She wanted to curl up and disappear from embarrassment.

Instead she lashed out at Kyle, calling him every vile name she could think of. "Get out of my room, you worm. Now. I never want to see you again." She ground her teeth together to keep from weeping.

"But, darlin', I love you."

"Love? *Love?* You don't know the meaning of love, Kyle Rutledge. Get out," she screamed. "Get out!"

"Okay, okay. I'm leaving. Take some time and cool down. I know I goofed up, and I'm sorry. But—"

She thrust her finger toward the exit. "Out!"

"I'm going. I'm going." Kyle gathered his belongings and left.

Irish collapsed in a heap of tears. She wept as if her heart were breaking. And it was.

She felt like such a fool.

She was leaving. Immediately. She couldn't bear facing Jackson or Matt or Pete or— Who else knew of the nasty game?

A new wave of humiliation washed over her.

Before she began weeping anew, she jumped to her feet and dragged her luggage from the closet.

Just as Irish slammed the trunk of the Mercedes, Mac strolled by. "Good morning," he said, "I've been out for an early walk. You're not leaving are you?"

She wiped her nose and tried to smile. "Yes, it's time for me to be on my way."

"Irish, what's wrong? Have you been crying?"

"Oh, no. I've discovered that I'm allergic to pine trees. Silly isn't it?"

"Forgive me if I don't believe you. You're very unhappy. Is there anything I can do to help?"

"No—" Then she remembered the state of her pocketbook and the state of the gas tank. She probably couldn't make it to the airport. "Well, I hate to ask, but could you loan me twenty dollars? I'll repay it as soon as I can."

He took a money clip from his pocket. "Here's a hundred, and you don't have to repay me. Do you need more?"

She hugged Mac and kissed his cheek. "No. You've been a dear. I wish we'd had time to become better friends."

He handed her his business card. "We'll make time. Call me when you're settled. I'll take you treasure hunting sometime."

Mac helped her into the driver's seat, and she waved goodbye as she headed for the highway. She didn't even slow down at Pete's. With only a brief stop for gas, she drove straight to Dallas, trying to figure out how she was going to come up with enough money to get a ticket back to Washington. Perhaps she should have borrowed the money from Mac, but her pride hadn't allowed it.

Where was her pride when she'd thought up this stupid stunt?

"Olivia," Irish said as she stood at the phone booth, "I don't want to go into the details right now. Please, just take Aunt Kate's silver candlesticks and hock them with Mr. Getz. As soon as you have the money, wire it to me so that I can buy a ticket home."

When she hung up, Irish sat down in the DFW terminal to wait until the money arrived.

Her stomach rumbled.

She hadn't eaten breakfast. After a bit of quick arithmetic, she decided that she could spare a few dollars of Mac's donation for food and went in search of a restaurant.

Her tray piled with bacon, eggs, toast, pancakes, cereal, milk, a banana, orange juice and coffee, she found a table for two and sat down. Some people couldn't eat when they were upset. Just the opposite with her. She could chew the bark off trees.

Halfway through her breakfast, the hair on the back of her neck prickled.

Glancing up, she saw Kyle striding straight toward her. She looked around for an escape route, but there wasn't one. If she couldn't avoid him, she would ignore him. She picked up her fork and cut into a pancake.

"Irish, darlin', I've been frantic trying to find you."

She ate the pancake, sipped from her coffee cup and didn't even look at him. He dragged up a chair and tried to talk to her. She merely looked him up and down as if he were some vile species of bug, then calmly peeled her banana and began slicing it over her cereal.

He grabbed her hand, pulled it to his mouth and chomped off the rest of the banana she held. "Dammit, Irish, listen to me."

"I can't hear you with your mouth full of banana."

He quickly swallowed. "I love you!" he bellowed. Several people tittered and turned to gawk.

"Shhh. Kyle, you're making a scene. People are staring. Go away."

"No, I'm not going away, and I don't care who knows it. I love you." He turned to the people in the restaurant. "I love her. I want to marry her. She's angry because I'm a millionaire. I ask you, is that fair?"

"Honey," a middle-aged redhead said, "if she doesn't want you, I'll take you."

"Marilyn!"

"Well, I would. He's a studmuffin. And rich to boot."

"Kyle, go away." Irish shaded her eyes with her hand and concentrated on her plate.

He rose and left. She didn't have time to be more than a tad regretful before he was back with armloads of flowers. The vendor from the flower cart followed with another armful.

Kyle laid the heaps of roses, carnations, mums and the rest at her feet. "I beseech you, love, accept these small tokens of my affection and forgive me for my transgressions." He fell to his knees and thrust out his arms theatrically.

Irish rolled her eyes heavenward and wished that

she could slither into a crack somewhere. "Shhhh," she hissed. "You're making a spectacle of us. Get up off your knees and go away."

"Not until you say that you'll forgive me."

She glared at him. "When hell freezes over." She dug into the cereal.

Kyle rose to his feet, and from the corner of her eye, she saw him talking to a kid with tattered clothes and a guitar case. She watched as Kyle peeled off a bill and handed it to the young man.

The kid squatted down and opened the guitar case. Kyle flagged another flower vendor, and soon he was back with another armful of roses and with the guitar player following behind singing an old Beatles song.

No wonder that a crowd gathered.

He knelt again beside her. "Irish, I love you with all my heart. Nobody, rich or poor, could ever love you as much as I do. My grandfather adores you. My cousins adore you. I adore you. My parents and my brother are sure to adore you. I will never, never lie to you again as long as I live. Please marry me, and everything I have is yours."

The guitar player sang louder.

Strangers in the crowd urged her to say yes.

She looked into his eyes, his gorgeous blue eyes, saw the love there, and was lost.

"Will you forgive me," he pleaded.

"Yes," she said softly.

"Did she say yes?" somebody in the crowd asked.

"Yes," she said more loudly.

The crowd cheered. Kyle grinned.

"Will you marry me?"

"Yes."

He pulled her into his arms and kissed her.

The crowd went wild. One would have thought that the Cowboys had won another Super Bowl.

Epilogue

The small Episcopal church had probably never before had so many millionaires under its roof at one time.

Kyle stood beside the altar waiting for the bride. Flint Durham, Kyle's best friend, stood beside him as best man. Smith would have had the honor, but he was laid up back in Texas with two broken legs. Standing as groomsmen were Jackson and Matt Crow, and as guests were every other member of the young millionaires club.

On the groom's side next to Kyle's parents, who were beaming, sat Cherokee Pete spiffed up in a tuxedo with his long braids. Behind them were Jackson and Matt's parents and Congresswoman Ellen Crow O'Hara, her husband and her three children.

On the bride's side, Irish's beautiful mother, Beverly, sat smiling and dabbing her eyes. Thankfully the Ellisons, the Rutledges, and the Crows got along like a house afire. In fact Pete had been urging Al Ellison to retire and move to Texas. There was plenty of room on his spread.

Kyle hoped that the Ellisons did decide to move to Texas and live near them. After some diligent soul-searching with Irish's help, he'd decided to go back into medicine. But this time he planned to work with children and others who had disfigurements rather than to do laser peels and nose jobs for the rich and famous. A position was already waiting for him in Dallas.

The music changed tempo and the full house stirred as the bridesmaids came down the aisle. First was Kim, looking very young and lovely in pale pink. Next came Olivia, regal in dusky rose. Both carried cascades of orchids.

Next, Eve Ellison, Irish's younger sister, walked slowly toward the altar. Eve wore a deep wine gown, and with her pale blond hair caught up in pearls instead of tied with a shoestring or some such, and wearing makeup instead of dirt smears, she was stunning.

The organ changed tempo again, and the guests rose and turned to greet the bride.

Kyle thought that his heart would burst when he saw Irish come down the aisle on her father's arm. He had insisted that she buy the most beautiful and lavish wedding gown in Dallas. She'd done well. It was exquisite.

And her beautiful face was radiant.

When Al surrendered his daughter to the groom, Kyle vowed silently that he would spend the rest of his life trying to make her happy and kept her safe and secure. Never again would she know fear.

When the final vows were said and they were pronounced man and wife, the kiss they shared rang clarion bells and sent skyrockets bursting over Akron.

They turned and hurried swiftly down the aisle. Behind them came Eve and Flint, then Olivia and Jackson, and lastly Kim and Matt.

As they hurried after the bride and groom, Jackson leaned over to Olivia and said, "Sugar, what say we blow the reception and you and me go to a little secluded place for dinner?"

Olivia looked at Jackson as if he were something nasty on her shoe. "In your dreams, buster. I'm not interested in anything you have to offer, and if you make another pass as me, I'll have you arrested."

*   *   *   *   *

And the Winner Is...
You!

...when you pick up these great titles
from our new promotion at your
favorite retail outlet this June!

Diana Palmer
The Case of the Mesmerizing Boss

Betty Neels
The Convenient Wife

Annette Broadrick
Irresistible

Emma Darcy
A Wedding to Remember

Rachel Lee
Lost Warriors

Marie Ferrarella
Father Goose

 HARLEQUIN® 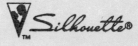 *Silhouette*®

Look us up on-line at: http://www.romance.net ATWI397-R

Take 4 bestselling love stories FREE

Plus get a FREE surprise gift!

Special Limited-time Offer

Mail to Silhouette Reader Service™

3010 Walden Avenue
P.O. Box 1867
Buffalo, N.Y. 14240-1867

YES! Please send me 4 free Silhouette Desire® novels and my free surprise gift. Then send me 6 brand-new novels every month, which I will receive months before they appear in bookstores. Bill me at the low price of $2.90 each plus 25¢ delivery and applicable sales tax, if any.* That's the complete price and a savings of over 10% off the cover prices—quite a bargain! I understand that accepting the books and gift places me under no obligation ever to buy any books. I can always return a shipment and cancel at any time. Even if I never buy another book from Silhouette, the 4 free books and the surprise gift are mine to keep forever.

225 BPA A3UU

Name	(PLEASE PRINT)	
Address	Apt. No.	
City	State	Zip

This offer is limited to one order per household and not valid to present Silhouette Desire® subscribers. *Terms and prices are subject to change without notice.
Sales tax applicable in N.Y.

UDES-696   ©1990 Harlequin Enterprises Limited

As seen on TV!
Free Gift Offer

With a Free Gift proof-of-purchase from any Silhouette® book, you can receive a beautiful cubic zirconia pendant.

This gorgeous marquise-shaped stone is a genuine cubic zirconia—accented by an 18" gold tone necklace.

(Approximate retail value $19.95)

Send for yours today...

compliments of ▼ *Silhouette*®

To receive your free gift, a cubic zirconia pendant, send us one original proof-of-purchase, photocopies not accepted, from the back of any Silhouette Romance™, Silhouette Desire®, Silhouette Special Edition®, Silhouette Intimate Moments® or Silhouette Yours Truly™ title available in February, March and April at your favorite retail outlet, together with the Free Gift Certificate, plus a check or money order for $1.65 U.S./$2.15 CAN. (do not send cash) to cover postage and handling, payable to Silhouette Free Gift Offer. We will send you the specified gift. Allow 6 to 8 weeks for delivery. Offer good until April 30, 1997 or while quantities last. Offer valid in the U.S. and Canada only.

Free Gift Certificate

Name: _____

Address: _____

City: _____ State/Province: _____ Zip/Postal Code: _____

Mail this certificate, one proof-of-purchase and a check or money order for postage and handling to: SILHOUETTE FREE GIFT OFFER 1997. In the U.S.: 3010 Walden Avenue, P.O. Box 9077, Buffalo NY 14269-9077. In Canada: P.O. Box 613, Fort Erie, Ontario L2Z 5X3.

FREE GIFT OFFER   084-KFD
ONE PROOF-OF-PURCHASE
To collect your fabulous FREE GIFT, a cubic zirconia pendant, you must include this original proof-of-purchase for each gift with the properly completed Free Gift Certificate.